THE LEFT BEHINDS

THE iPHONE THAT SAVED GEORGE WASHINGTON

THE LEFT BEHINDS

THE iPHONE THAT SAVED GEORGE WASHINGTON

DAVID POTTER

CROWN BOOKS
FOR YOUNG READERS
NEW YORK

Text copyright © 2015 by David Potter
Cover art copyright © 2015 by C. F. Payne

All rights reserved. Published in the United States by Crown Books for Young Readers, an imprint of Random House Children's Books, a division of Random House LLC, a Penguin Random House Company, New York.

Crown and the colophon are registered trademarks of Random House LLC.

Visit us on the Web! randomhousekids.com

Educators and librarians, for a variety of teaching tools, visit us at RHTeachersLibrarians.com

Library of Congress Cataloging-in-Publication Data
Potter, David.
The Left Behinds : the iPhone that saved George Washington / David Potter.—
First edition.
pages cm
Summary: Three students, Mel, Bev, and Brandon, left behind at their prestigious school during Christmas break, find themselves in 1776 New Jersey with General George Washington dead at their feet, and twelve-year-old Mel must find a way, using his iPhone, to set things right.
ISBN 978-0-385-39056-9 (hc) — ISBN 978-0-385-39057-6 (glb) —
ISBN 978-0-385-39058-3 (ebook)
[1. Time travel—Fiction. 2. Adventure and adventurers —Fiction. 3. iPhone (Smartphone) —Fiction. 4. Washington, George, 1732–1799 — Fiction. 5. Franklin, Benjamin, 1706–1790 — Fiction. 6. New Jersey —History —Revolution, 1775–1783 — Fiction.] I. Title.
PZ7.P85173Lef 2015
[Fic]—dc23
2014006650

Printed in the United States of America
10 9 8 7 6 5 4 3 2 1
First Edition

Random House Children's Books supports the First Amendment and celebrates the right to read.

For Cindy, Thomas, and Charlie

To Franklin School,

Huzzah!

Dan Poth

To Franklin

School!

Horton!

Dan Dodd

CONTENTS

WE FIND OURSELVES IN A
STRANGE SITUATION. . . .

ONE

I'D LIKE TO START at the beginning—believe me—but the problem is I don't know when it began and I don't know when it will end. I only know the middle, which is now, or more specifically ten minutes ago, when someone shot General George Washington stone-cold dead.

And today is Christmas Day.

"This is not cool," says Brandon. "George Washington is only, you know, the Father of the Country."

Bev says: "Really, Brandon? You think?"

We're in a stable, I guess you'd call it. This little house for horses. There are stacks of hay, saddles hanging up on a wall, bunches of rope, and a god-awful stench. We're peering into one of the horse stalls, where General George Washington is lying dead. Wearing his greatcoat, and under that his buff-and-blue uniform. Black boots up to his knees. In the middle of his chest is a large red bullet hole.

I don't have to tell you what *that* looks like, do I?

It's Brandon, me, and Beverly. Beverly is the only Beverly I've ever met. I know Emmas, Avas, Chloes, Abigails, and Olivias, but no other Beverly. It's a name that's gone out of fashion, like Herbert or Phyllis or Marge.

Bev's sort of the smart one, though. And Brandon's sort of the dumb one. He speaks with a slow slacker drawl and brags that he's failing every class, but Brandon's no dummy. He just likes to play it that way, for the laughs he gets.

None of us are laughing now. Before us, dead as ye olde doornail, is the guy who's supposed to become the first president of These United States.

They're even going to name the capital after him.

And the plan for tonight is a little surprise raid on a bunch of Hessians that are camped out in Trenton, across the Delaware River. Which they're hoping will turn the tide, because up until now, things haven't been going so great for this little thing they've been having called a revolution. As a matter of fact, the whole deal was close to being a total fail. Washington had lost every battle he'd been in up to this point. The British had taken New York, kicked the Continental Army out of New Jersey, and were on their way to conquer Philadelphia. Worst of all, Washington's men were set to pack up and clear out—

their enlistments were over at the end of the year, which was, like, seven days away.

So for Washington, it was one of those now-or-never kind of situations. Do something now, or get hanged later. And, as far as the revolution goes, that would be the end of that. We've learned all about it at school. Or at least we learned how things are *supposed* to turn out. Washington's Crossing of the Delaware was only supposed to be, you know, like the most important *turning point* of the entire Revolutionary War. I mean, if it didn't succeed the United States wouldn't even *exist*. But it's going to be pretty tough for anything to turn out *right* if the main guy happens to be—you know. Dead.

"Man," Brandon says. "Would you check this out?" He leans down to make a closer examination.

"Brandon, watch it," Bev says. "Don't touch . . ."

"The evidence?" Brandon says. "What do you think this is, *CSI* or something?" Then he grabs a straw—a *piece* of straw, that is, from the ground—and dips it in.

In . . . you know. The bullet hole.

Which kind of grosses us out. And kind of fascinates us at the same time. Brandon holds up the straw. It's red now. Glistening with warm red blood.

Then he asks the question we've all been thinking. "Is this . . . um . . . body . . . really George Washington? *The* George Washington? Or is it one of those reenactor dudes?" Now, this question might not make a bit of sense to you, but it makes perfect sense to us. Kind of.

"I have a very strange feeling," I say. "I have the strangest feeling I've ever had in my whole life. I *know* that's not a reenactor dude. Guys, I am one hundred percent positive we are looking at the *real* George Washington himself."

"Yeah, well, let's check," Brandon says, and reaches into his pocket. He pulls out a crumpled dollar bill. He unfolds, looks at it, and then looks at the face on the ground. "It's gotta be him," Brandon says. "It's a perfect match. He's the real deal, all right. But he's also dead. Way dead."

"Boys," says Bev. This is how Bev always talks to us, as if we're just one blobby entity, not two distinct individuals. And trust me when I tell you, we couldn't be more different. We don't form any kind of entity. We're not even *friends,* exactly. We've all just been kind of . . . thrown together.

The Left Behinds, is what we're called. We know that's what they call us, because we heard them. In the Dining Hall. One Dining Hall lady said to another Dining Hall lady, "Don't worry about it, we'll just have leftovers for the *Left Behinds.*" Then they both cackled up a storm, it was so funny. They stopped mid-cackle when they saw me and Bev looking at them, holding our lunch trays, and ever since then they've had trouble meeting our eyes, as if *we've* done something to be ashamed of. Look—our parents are *busy,* all right? They're really, like, *successful* people, okay? And it's not as if we haven't been home for the Christmas holidays before. I've been to twelve of them, all in a row.

"Boys," Bev says. "I don't think we should be messing around with this. As a matter of fact, I'm beginning to think we should get ourselves away from here. As fast as humanly possible."

"Away from where?" Brandon says. "This place, or this century?"

You see? I told you Brandon wasn't so dumb.

TWO

M Y NAME IS MEL. It's not really Mel, which would be short for Melvin, which is even more old-fashioned than Beverly or Herbert, but that's what people call me. I'll tell you this much: It's my initials. M and E and L. But I'm not going to say my real name. You might have heard of it, because it's the same name my father has, and I'm pretty sure you've heard of *him*. He's super busy, remember? And successful. So I'll go by Mel, and let's leave it at that.

You might have heard of Bev's mom too. She's a star of stage and screen. Currently appearing six nights a week and twice on Sundays in a play in Los Angeles. Which means Bev has to stay behind with us, because Mommy Dearest doesn't want her daughter around when she's "performing." Which, according to Bev, is only morning, noon, and night.

Her father is a famous actor dude from Argentina, but he's like *completely* out of the picture, and always has been. I found this out after Googling Bev's mom, but don't tell anyone, because Googling people behind their backs is so uncool. Everyone does it, though. What's even more uncool is getting caught.

I know all this about Bev because of Google and because I tend to overhear her when she's on her cell phone—I mean, it's not like she talks to *me* at all. Bev, says Bev, *hates* all of it: Broadway, Los Angeles, stardom, paparazzi, TMZ, *ET,* the whole *celebrity* thing. It's all so totally *pointless*. And now that her mom's on the downslope of her career—the play's in *Los Angeles,* after all, not Broadway—there's less and less paparazzi, TMZ, and *ET.* So her mom is now becoming a *former* celebrity, which is even worse.

If you're thinking I have a thing for Bev, you would be wrong. She *interests* me is all it is, okay? It's not like I'm *obsessing* about her or anything. She just happens to be the kind of girl who's hard *not* to notice.

For example: do I normally pay attention to what girls wear?

I do not.

Except for Bev.

Because you never know what she's going to come up with. Like her attitude is *clothes?* What could *possibly* be less important?

She's not *consistent,* is the problem. So it's tough to get a fix on her. One day she's Little Miss Preppy. The next, Miss Slobberina. Kind of like she just throws on whatever happens to be handy.

That's what the guys do, but we always throw on the same old stuff. Like now, I'm wearing jeans, sneakers, some T-shirt I found on the floor of my room, and a jacket. Brandon's wearing a red hat that has a picture of a snarling wolf on it, with its teeth bared. Brandon will tell you, if you ask, that it's not a wolf, it's a *lobo,* which is the Spanish word for *wolf* and happens to be the mascot of the University of New Mexico. Classy, right?

Bev, on the other hand, is wearing some pink jacket and earmuffs. Just in case it was going to be cold, which it isn't, but that's Bev: practical. Prepared.

Bev is not about looking good, you have to understand. Oh no.

That stuff is all just so . . . so . . . *common.*

Gets in the way of her *agenda.* She's announced that she's going to be a biochemist one day and find the cure for cancer. That, or save the lives of newborns as a pediatric neurosurgeon. Maybe both. Anything that is useful, practical, and as far away from Hollywood as possible.

And as far away from us.

I know she's awfully put-upon to have to spend her Christmas holiday with the likes of Brandon and me, but still. You try to talk to her, and it takes maybe three seconds before she cuts you dead and says, "Okay, okay, what's your point?"

So like right now, Bev doesn't want to stop and think things through. Or ask any difficult questions, such as, how is it that three kids from the Fredericksville School—or should I say the *prestigious* Fredericksville School, because no one ever lets you forget it—happen to be in a smelly stable standing over the most important guy in our nation's history? Who happens to be *dead*?

Who, apparently, was shot in the chest like *ten* minutes ago?

And if this is the real George Washington, and not some lame reenactor dude, that would mean what? That we've somehow been *transported* to 1776?

Which would not be possible. Right? So there's absolutely no way, no how, that this dead guy in the stall is the real deal. So that should settle it.

And yet . . . and yet . . . why do I keep thinking that he *is* real, and I'm wrong? "All right," I speak up. "It's about time we start freaking out. This is, like, a crime scene, and you're not supposed to mess with anything. Bev? What do you think we should do?"

We all sort of inventory our surroundings. And we notice some deeply weird stuff. Like one, there are no horses in this so-called horse stable. And two, there's snow outside. And there's snow on General George Washington's boots. But not on our own boots and sneakers.

There was absolutely, positively no snow where we came from. We don't have snowy Christmases anymore. Haven't you heard about global warming?

So . . . maybe you can forgive us. For having a little

brain fritz. It's really . . . kind of difficult . . . to process. . . .
Here. There. Now. Then.

Now is here, but there was then, but now is 1776 and
then was the twenty-first century?

Huh?

We should stop and think this thing through. Before
we do anything stupid.

But then we hear something. Trampling through the
snow.

People.

Coming our way.

Talking. Which focuses our minds and stops us from
asking ourselves any more dumb questions.

We notice the stable has two entrances—one on the
left and one on the right.

It takes us about one-quarter millisecond to decide to
go right, one-quarter to start moving, and the rest of the
millisecond is all we need to get out of there.

And into nothing but snow. A big, vast expanse of
white. Brandon leads the way, like a fullback rushing up
the middle of the line, making a path for Bev and me.
The talking people start running after us.

We can hear them, trampling around back there. Running through snow, in case you didn't know, is a pretty
noisy activity.

And then the people start yelling at us. Yelling, like,
really, really loud.

And then I notice something funny. It figures that I

would notice it, since I was the only kid taking German. Bev takes French, Brandon takes Spanish, but I take German, 'cause my dad told me to.

These dudes are yelling, *"Diebe, Diebe! Stoppen Sie sofort! Stoppen Sie sofort!"* Since I've been paying attention in German class, this means something like, "Thieves, thieves! Stop at once!"

But we aren't, so we don't.

THREE

As I said, I take German 'cause Dad told me to. Last year I complied with one hundred percent of what he said.

This year? Maybe eighty percent. Maybe more like sixty. I know the compliance factor has been sliding downhill, but then my dad is a *demanding* kind of guy.

It's got him to where he is, which is pretty high up there. And of course he went to the Fredericksville School himself, back in the day. As did his dad, and his dad's dad.

It's kind of a family thing. *Legacy* is the term I think I'm supposed to use. So the family legacy is we go to the Fredericksville School, and while there, we rule. I know my dad and my dad's dad, etc., ruled, because I can see their names up on the captain's boards in the Nelson Field House. This place is humongous and must have cost twenty million bucks. It's designed so as soon as you walk in, you say, "Whoa." There are pools, ice hockey rinks, basketball courts, and the main field, which is, like, six acres. All indoors. Two floors. And lining the walls are these gorgeous wood boards, with gold lettering, with the names of all the illustrious captains of yesteryear's teams embossed on them for eternity. My grandfather was captain of the fencing team in 1945. And Dad was captain of the lacrosse team in both 1981 *and* 1982. He was also in the choir, the jazz band, the art club, and the debate team, and he spent a summer in Mali, which is in Africa, on a mission to help the poor.

When he found out I hadn't taken his orders, I mean *instructions,* I mean *advice,* to go out for soccer, join no less than three clubs, try to get the lead in the school play, and finagle a position on the school paper to make sure my exploits were duly recorded—when he found out I had done none of it, he blew a cork *and* a gasket.

"Son," said Dad. "Are you going to be a potted plant, someone who just sits there, for Pete's sake, or are you going to be somebody? Because it's one or the other, son. There's no getting around it. You're either a potted plant or you're a somebody. And if you want to be somebody, son, you're going to have to stand up. Raise your hand. Step forward. Take a chance. *Count.* You want to count for something, don't you, son? You want to be *somebody*, right? You don't just want to be a *potted plant*, do you?"

"No, Dad," I said. "No, I do not want to be a potted plant."

He continued fuming and spewing until he was called away by Something Important. That's the thing about Dad and his tirades. They never go on too long because he's got people always tugging on his shirt to get his attention onto something else. Which is usually okay by me. You see, my dad just happens to be one of those guys who's a little bit *much*, you know what I mean? My mom says he gets in your grill, which is to say he likes to stand about two inches from your face, like he's arguing a call with an umpire.

It puts some people off. After a while, it even put my mom off, which is why they got divorced last year.

She did tell me not to take it personally, though, because, she said, *it had nothing to do with me.* Then she decided to take a trip. A two-year trip, up, down, and around the world.

So this is why, if you really want to know, we weren't having a family Christmas this year, and why I was staying at the Fredericksville School with the Left Behinds. Okay? It really wasn't because Dad is so busy, or so important. It's because just the two of us, with some sad little Christmas tree, would have seemed so Loser City. And the last thing Dad was going to let me witness was him losing at anything.

See, Dad is a well-known guy, like I said. In certain

circles. He's been on the covers of magazines, on the front page of the *New York Times* one time. He's not an everyday *People* magazine celebrity like Bev's mom, but he is *known*, all right.

My dad's the guy who lost a billion bucks.

Or maybe it was ten billion.

He used to work for one of those big investment banks. You know, the ones that are too big to *fail*.

Which is exactly what he did.

I don't know all the particulars. If I knew them, I wouldn't understand anyway. But somehow his *desk* placed all these *bets* and then they got *burned*. And whatever this desk thing was, he was in charge of it.

He was held up as an example of *everything* that was wrong with Wall Street, the financial system, and the American way. If you Google him, he'll come up, like, about two *million* times. And he's a guy who used to think he was the biggest winner that ever walked upon the planet Earth. So he's having a tough time *adjusting*.

To losing anything, let alone his own wife. But he's still chock-full of advice, whenever he does get a chance to speak to me. Though at the moment, I'm not sure what he'd tell me to do: keep running, or *Stoppen Sie sofort*.

Since he can't weigh in, we're running.

Brandon takes a hard right, and we follow. He had been going straight into woods, where the snow is, like, three feet high, but he must have seen where it leveled out to the right, and thataway he went.

It does level out. We come to kind of a path. There

are other buildings around—a stone farmhouse, another smaller stone building next to that. And right in front of us, two men in spiffy blue uniforms. Did you hear what I said?

Spiffy blue uniforms.

Soldiers, in other words.

Real ones. Not reenactor dudes.

It's not hard to tell the difference. They *smell,* for one thing. Two, they've got snow on their boots. Not new snow like us. Frozen stuff. Like they've been out here for days.

Three, they have large white sashes across their chests, epaulets on their shoulders, and weird gold cone things on their heads. I know right away who they are: Hessians. German soldiers for hire, who rented themselves out to the British. I know who they are because I've read about them. I never expected to see any Hessians for myself, though. Especially not up close and personal.

They don't look overfriendly, these Hessian dudes.

They ain't smiling, for one thing.

And two, they've got muskets, which are raised, ready, and pointed straight at us.

FOUR

We stop. Behind us, the guys who've been shouting, who followed the same swath Brandon made in the snow, catch up. There are two of them, but they're not wearing uniforms. Just regular eighteenth-century farmer clothes.

You know that time travel idea I had? Which I said was impossible?

Guess what. Maybe I'm wrong.

One of the guys dressed as a farmer speaks up. In English, but with a super-thick German accent. "You are trespassing," this guy says. The first thing I think is, *He sounds* exactly *like Arnold You-Know-Who in* The Terminator. "This is private property. You have no business of being here."

This guy is butt-ugly. He's also short, which makes him even uglier. His face is all kind of squashed in, like he ate something sour and can't get the taste out of his mouth. Plus his nose is crooked. It leans to his right, our left. Someone should have told him to wear a hat to hide his hair, which is scurvy-looking and knotted, like rope. When he leans in to talk to us, we lean back. Like way, way back.

"Dude," says Brandon. "Chillax, will ya?" And then Brandon wipes the air in front of him, like he's trying to get rid of a stench.

"You have no business of being here," the guy says again. "Ve shoot you and kill you if ve vant."

"You're not shooting anyone," Bev says, stepping forward. And she's got an attitude. Her attitude is this: My mom is a big star, buster. Who the heck are you? "Or should I say you're not shooting anyone *else*. There happens to be a dead man in the barn back there. Who we have reason to believe happens to be a most important person. Do you know anything about this? If this is your property, then you are most definitely responsible." Bev pauses, and then points her finger. "Each and every one of you."

The guy takes a pistol from the pocket of his jacket, lifts the thing up, cocks it, and points it straight at me. But he doesn't shoot. Instead he starts to notice things. Like our clothes. Our jeans. Our sneakers. The snarling wolf on Brandon's hat. Bev's checkered scarf and stylin' winter jacket. And probably, like, twenty other things. So we watch as the guy tallies them up and comes to some sort of conclusion: we're *different*.

Like, *way* different.

He says something in German to the others. Too fast for me to catch the words. But I think, by the tone of his voice, he must have said something like this: Guys, let's be careful here. Very, very careful. Because these kids seem awfully strange. . . .

FIVE

THE TWO UNIFORMED GUYS in front of us, and the two nonuniformed guys behind us, all start talking to each other at once. In German. So it's kind of a standoff for, like, a really, really, really long time. Like for maybe five, ten seconds.

No one knows what to do. They must be thinking we're way weird, and that's for sure what we're thinking about them.

Let's just take one thing common to us all. Or thirty-two things for each of us, and maybe half that for them. I'm talking about *teeth*. How often do you think about teeth? You think about your own when you floss and brush, and you think about somebody else's only when you notice something wrong or funny or weird.

Oh yeah, one other thing: if you have braces, like I still do, you think about what a pain in the butt they are and you can't wait to get them off.

So that's us: two sets of bright-white smiles, plus me, Mr. Steel Cage Mouth.

Those guys maybe have three good teeth among 'em. The rest are rotten little stubby things. Gray, and full of gunk. And I would bet you five million dollars not one of them has ever swished around a mouthful of Listerine either, though God knows they could use it.

Then we hear a funny little sound. An electronic sound, a micro three-chord melody that the three of us hear a hundred times a day. And think nothing of it.

But a sound the four of them have *never* heard. Never, but never.

It's my iPhone. Which I've been holding this whole entire time.

It's what we do. It's probably what you do. You hold the thing in your hand, because you use it so much. God forbid you miss something, right?

It's the same deal, by the way, with Brandon and Bev. We're holding on to our iPhones, like they'll save us. Then Brandon does something unexpected. Brandon's a funny kid. He's kind of big, kind of goofy, and I know for a fact that he had long hair—like, down to his shoulders—before he came to school, because I saw a picture of him once. He's also the only boy I know who wears *bracelets*. You know, on his wrists. Two on the left and one on the right. I think they're Native American things, but then Brandon's from New Mexico, of all places. He's a Left Behind because his mom went spiritual on him and moved to an ashram, where she's been trying to get in touch with The Universe. But she sent her boy to the Fredericksville School so he could have a proper East Coast education with all the trimmings. His family has something to do with the oil business, though I think his dad passed away. And while his mom gets to go spiritual, Brandon gets to go to a fancy school. They made him cut his hair, and they made him buy new clothes. New packaging, but same kid. It doesn't work even if you dress him up with a tie and blue blazer.

Oh yeah, and there's another thing about Brandon. Besides nearly failing every class, he doesn't like to follow orders. I'm sure he squawked about the haircut. He gives all his teachers a hard time whenever he can. And right now, he decides to mess around with Mr. Butt-Ugly and Company. He holds up his iPhone. Then he points it at Butt-Ugly and snaps off a picture.

The German guys—soldiers and farmers alike—aren't sure what this is all about, but they don't seem to like it. They kind of take a step back.

Maybe we're on to something. Maybe *we're* armed and dangerous, because each one of us has an iPhone of our very own. There's just one thing. "I hope this isn't going to be a problem," I say, looking down at my cell phone.

Of course, I didn't bother to recharge it anytime recently. "But I'm running low on power. I'm, like, at ten percent. When did that happen?"

Which leads directly to my next question: any chance of outlets, here in 1776?

SIX

THE GUY WHO SPEAKS English, Mr. Butt-Ugly—who's the same guy holding his pistol straight at my head—asks a question. Probably the first thing that came to his mind, and all things considered, it's not such a dumb question.

"Vhat," he says, nodding to the iPhone in Brandon's hand, "is dis?"

Brandon turns his iPhone around and shows the dude the picture he just took.

If you've never seen a grown man spooked before—I mean, like, totally, completely, one hundred percent freaked—then you've got to go someplace and find a guy who's not only never seen a photo before, but never even knew of the *existence* of such a thing. The dude completely loses it. First his eyes pop a socket. Next his mouth gapes open. Then he lowers his arm, the one holding the pistol, and takes five steps backward, like he's propelled by some force and can't help himself.

His other arm flails around—in midair—as if trying to wave something away.

Brandon points his iPhone at the other farmer, who has seen what it did to Butt-Ugly. This guy doesn't wait to see the results—he just turns and starts running back to the stable.

"*Teufel!*" the guy screams. "*Teufel!*"

Now, I can't say I've heard the word before, but I think I know what it means. It means, I'm pretty sure, "devil."

I don't know about you, but I think it's kind of cool to have somebody call me a devil.

And then run away from me as fast as they possibly can.

It gives me this weird kind of feeling, like I actually have some *power*.

It doesn't matter that I don't have a gun, a musket, a bazooka, or a flamethrower.

What I do have is a *belief*. Not mine, but theirs. Which just shows you which one is stronger: a belief or a gun. We're the Apple Artillery. Two black ones, one white. We hold them aloft like they're death ray guns and watch as all the German dudes scatter.

It's almost funny, till I notice on mine that I have a message. A text.

Which doesn't compute for a second, because how

could a text . . . you know . . . from now to then . . . I mean, from then to now . . . be sent? Or received?

It's from my teacher. Mr. Hart. American History.

And then I start to remember a couple of things. It's like a fog starting to break up. Like: isn't this whole . . . expedition . . . part of some lame school trip? For us Left Behinds? And isn't Mr. Hart our sorry teacher who got stuck with us for the Christmas holidays, because maybe he himself had nothing better to do either?

And didn't Mr. Hart say, this very morning, "Kids, today we're going to the reenactment of Washington's crossing of the Delaware, which they do every Christmas at Washington Crossing State Park."

Bev and Brandon rolled their eyes. Me? I was kind of into it, if you want to know the truth. I have no defense. I'm a history nerd, which is only totally uncool.

"What's the matter, Mel?" Brandon says. "See something funny?"

"I got a text," I say. "From Mr. Hart."

"Yeah? What does he want?"

I read it myself first.

Where R U? it says.

I read the message aloud, and all of us stop and puzzle over it.

And then I get another one. The same three-chord micro melody.

R U lost?

I read this one aloud, too. We take a glance around. I guess the answer would be yes and no.

"You have to tell him something," Bev says. "He might be worried about us."

"What should I say?"

"Tell him we've taken a little detour," Brandon says. "The scenic route."

"I think I'll tell him we'll be right back," I say.

"Will we?" says Bev. She's worried all of a sudden. Which isn't something you see from Bev very often. She's always so sure of herself. Her being worried gets me worried.

"Let's hope so," I say, and type it in. I notice that I'm down to nine percent power.

But we have other things to think about at the moment. Immediate, like, issues. They've run, the Germans have, but they haven't left. They've *taken positions*. To the left of us, and to the right of us. Muskets at the ready. They're maybe seventy or eighty yards away. They've *fallen back* to a *secure line*.

It's easy to throw around military terms when you've learned a few. I used to tell people I was playing Xbox when I was really watching the History Channel.

"Boys," Bev says. "Behind us is nothing but woods."

"And in front of us," Brandon says, "is nothing but muskets."

"That one guy," I say. "The guy who speaks English. He's looking at us. Through a telescope ... Spyglass? Whatever they call those things."

"He's curious," Bev says. "He wants to know what our phones are all about."

"Maybe," I say, "he wants one for himself."

"For what?" says Brandon. "So he can take pictures?"

"Everybody," I say, "wants to get their hands on an iPhone. It's just natural."

"Boys," Bev says again. "What's the plan here? Backward? Forward? Left, right? 'Cause I don't know about you guys, but I'm getting cold. My feet are, like, frozen solid."

"Maybe," says Brandon, "we should go back to the stable. It was a lot warmer in there."

That's Brandon for you. He's always for the easiest way, but not necessarily the best way.

"The stable's a dumb idea, Brandon," says Bev. "They'll corner us in that place. Then what?"

"Then I don't know," Brandon says. "Mel, what do you think?"

"I think these guys," I say, nodding to the Germans still arrayed in front of us, "must be the guys who killed Washington." It occurs to me—and probably to Bev and to Brandon—that if these are the guys who killed George Washington, they probably have it in them to kill us as well.

"Maybe they did," Bev says. "So do we stay here? Do we run for it? Plus, I have something else on my mind. If you have to know."

"Which is what?" I say.

"Um. I'm wondering if there's a bathroom anywhere nearby," Bev says.

Brandon gives her the bad news. "There aren't any, Bev," he says. "Bathrooms with flush toilets haven't been invented yet. They use outhouses."

"Or pots and pans," I say. "Next to the bed."

"Terrific," Bev says. "Just terrific. Can someone tell me what we're doing here? And how do we get back?"

No one can. But then our English-speaking, spyglass-holding German friend starts waving a flag. A white one.

As if *those guys* are surrendering to *us*.

SEVEN

Now some of this is starting to come back to me. Our school closes down for the Christmas holiday from December 22 to January 2. Ninety-nine point nine percent of the kids go home—or go someplace, anyway—for the holidays.

Every year—so we're told—a handful of kids can't go home. 'Cause their parents are, you know, too *busy*. Too *successful*. So they make *arrangements*. To have the school take care of the kids from December 22 to January 2.

They didn't tell me who else was going to be left behind—and I sure as heck didn't ask anyone—so when the big day came, for a while I thought I was going to be the only one. Parents came and got their kids, and everyone was so Christmassy with hearty good cheer and season's tidings, it made me want to puke.

I was told to wait in my room.

Then—after the place cleared out, so no one would notice—I was told to go to the Dining Hall.

And there was Bev.

Somewhat *peeved,* as usual. In a theatrical kind of way. Because Bev can't just sit there and be peeved like anyone else, you see. The whole *world* has to know. And thanks to her mom, and her gene pool, Bev is a complete natural when it comes to letting the world know how she feels about something.

But—to be completely honest here—seeing that Bev was a Left Behind sort of . . . sort of . . . sparked things up a bit, at least from my point of view.

I mean, like, *everyone* at school knows who Bev is. She hadn't so much as said two words to me all year, though. We weren't in any of the same classes. Though I kind of was aware of her schedule. I mean, when I had English, Bev had math. When I had American history, she had biology. Look, I just happened to know this, so don't start reading into it. I have a good memory, all right? And I'm a guy who notices stuff.

But I will say that when I saw Bev in the Dining Hall, I wasn't a hundred percent disappointed.

Okay, for a second, a split second, and no longer than that, I thought, *How utterly convenient.*

Together at last.

I tried to start a conversation. I said something lame, like "Stuck here too?"

And Bev said: "Yeah. What's your point?" Which pretty much ended that effort, dead on the spot.

Fifteen minutes later Brandon rambled in, and our little group was complete. Mr. Hart laid out the program for us. Fun trips, here and there.

One day we went to the American Museum of Natural History in New York. Which was fun, except we've been there, like, fifty times already.

One day we went to an indoor water park.

And then this morning, Christmas Day, the grand announcement: the Washington Crossing the Delaware thingy. A bunch of reenactor dudes—generally speaking, weird overweight guys dressed up in Revolutionary War garb who are probably accountants and sales guys in real life—parade around and then get into four or five boats and row themselves across the Delaware, from Pennsylvania to New Jersey. Holiday crowds line the banks on both sides and give the accountants and sales guys a big "Huzzah, huzzah!" when they make it over.

Then we were supposed to go back to school and have a lovely Christmas Day feast, with a proper turkey and fixings, and exchange a bunch of gifts, if we had any to give or receive. If any of our parents had secretly sent gifts to us, they'd be forked over.

All right.

Okay.

This much I remember now. And Mr. Hart, our history teacher, was the oddball who had to go with us on every one of our little day trips, and didn't get to go home to any family he might have had somewhere. So this morning, Mr. Hart drove us over in the school van. Bev rode shotgun, Brandon and I sat in the back. I stared out the window, and told myself that this probably wouldn't be the worst Christmas I would ever have in my life. It was the worst one up until now, for sure, but I still had a long way to go.

The ride over wasn't much fun. It was, in fact, basically dead silent the whole way.

The pretty but snooty one in the front, the slacker dude in the back, and me.

Like I said, none of us are exactly friends.

We didn't, you know, talk to each other and stuff like that.

We were just thrown together, and told to make the best of it.

We are the Left Behinds.

So what do we know about *surrender flags*?

Have any of us ever been surrendered to before?

I think not. What the heck is the *protocol*? The correct *procedure*?

Are we supposed to say "Okay, no prob" and wave 'em in? Then what do we do?

Grab their muskets?

At a time like this, we wouldn't actually mind having Mr. Hart around, even though he's kind of dorky.

"What do we do?" I say. "How do we know it's not a trick?"

The English-speaking dude—Mr. Butt-Ugly—is still waving his white flag. Back and forth, back and forth.

"I like really, really need to find a bathroom," says Bev.

"I think," I say, "that we ought to tell them to put down their muskets. And then come forward."

"With their hands up?" Brandon asks. "Or behind their heads?"

"I think with their hands up," I say. "Who knows what they got in those high hats of theirs."

Brandon does the honors. He's got the biggest voice, and he lets it rip.

EIGHT

"LAY YOUR MUSKETS DOWN!" Brandon shouts. "And come out with your hands up!"

Then we all kind of snicker. I mean, just how often do you get a chance to say something like that?

Mr. Butt-Ugly yells back, "Ve vant to talk! Ve don't vant to surrender. Ve propose von hour truce."

This is a curveball. No one's sure what to make of it.

"An hour-long truce?" I say. "What's that going to get us?"

"It's going to get us an hour," says Bev. "Maybe we can agree, if it's someplace warm. With a bathroom."

"There are no bathrooms, Bev," Brandon and I say at practically the same time.

Brandon checks behind us, then to the left, then to the

right. All dramatic-like. Then he says: "Guys, what options do we have here? I'm starting to get cold too. And I don't see any place to . . . to run to . . . around here. What time is it, anyway?"

We glance at our phones. It's 2:02 p.m., Wednesday, December 25.

And I'm down to eight percent power.

Then I get another text. Again from Mr. Hart.

I read aloud: *Did you go to the basement of the Taylorsville General Store?*

"Did we?" I ask.

"Did we what?" says Brandon.

"Go to the basement of the Taylorsville General Store. It was off to the side, remember? It had its own entrance."

And then we think. All of us, at the same time, about the same subject, which is probably something that doesn't happen often. Certainly not in any classroom we've been in recently.

"I think we did," says Brandon. "Something's coming back."

"We did," says Bev. "Of course we did. I'm not surprised that all of you disremember, but then your attention spans are rather limited. It was your idea, Brandon. If you recall, you dared us. Like we were all a bunch of third-graders."

"That's right," I say, snapping my fingers. "We were bored, we went to the Taylorsville General Store, we saw this old guy scurry out of the basement, and Brandon, you said, 'What in heck is this geezer up to?' Remember? Then you said, 'Let's find out.' And you said we wouldn't do it, not even on a dare."

"But we did," Bev says. "The door wasn't locked. There were no lights. There was a staircase. The basement was black."

"We used our iPhones," says Brandon. "To light the way."

"So let me tell him," I say. I tap back a single word: *Yes*.

It doesn't take long for Mr. Hart to answer. A couple seconds, maybe. Which sort of sticks in my mind, because, um, how can this *happen*?

Are we *texting* each other?

Across what—almost 240 years?

But before my brain explodes, I read aloud his text. *Did anything . . . unusual happen?*

I type back: *Kind of.*

Then he texts: *R U OK?*

I send this: *We're fine.*

Mr. Hart: *R U all together?*

Me: *Yes.*

We're gathered around my iPhone, naturally, all of us reading his texts as they come in. "Why don't we just call the dude?" Brandon says. "Tell him to pick us up with the van?"

"Not a bad idea," I say, and try, but no dice. Not even a dial tone. "Something is extremely weird about this," I say. "Did someone mess around with my phone?"

No one answers, but Mr. Hart sends another text. *I'm afraid you may find yourselves in a very strange situation. Don't panic! We'll get you back.*

OK, I type. And then: *Anytime soon?*

He answers: *One question: has anything changed?*

Like what? I say.

Answer the question, he says, annoyed. I can tell. Mr. Hart is easy to read, in person or by text.

"What should I tell him," I say. "The truth?"

"Go ahead," says Brandon. "Blow the dude's mind. Why should we be the ones having all the fun?"

No dissent, not from anyone, though now Bev is looking super peeved. I think it's more the bathroom thing, though.

So I go for it. *Someone killed George Washington. Pretty sure it was him.*

He types back, and now I'm sure he's annoyed, because Mr. Hart never misspells anything. *R U kiding?*

NO, I say, all caps.

He returns the favor. *WHO????*

HESSIANS, I type back.

Then there's a pause. A long, long pause. It's almost like Mr. Hart is consulting with somebody on the other side.

Finally this: *Power down! You MUST not lose power. Reconvene in one hour for further instructions! Be safe!*

I turn my phone off, and look around. Be safe? Easy for him to say.

The thing is, Mr. Hart's texts are kind of hard to process, because we have these German guys seventy, eighty yards away. Who are waiting for our answer.

To their one-hour truce request.

"What do we say to those guys?" I say, nodding to the Hessians.

"I don't trust them," Bev says. "Not for a minute. We're witnesses. And I don't care what year it is, there's only one thing you do with witnesses: you get rid of them."

"We didn't witness anything," Brandon says. "We didn't actually see anything *happen*."

"We saw a dead guy in a horse stall," Bev says. "One minute later, we see these guys. Two plus two, Brandon. Add it up. It's not hard."

"And that dead guy just happens to be," I say, "General George Washington. So they have every reason in the world to want to get rid of us."

"Boys," Bev says, and we're like, *Enough already with the bathroom.* But Bev says something else. "Boys, two things. One, if I'm not mistaken, Washington wasn't supposed to get killed today. And this would have a pretty big effect on how things are supposed to turn out, don't you think? So that's a big problem. And second, I'll be right back. You guys stay here. And don't turn around."

We get it. We have enough to think about, so we don't think about Bev. We have to figure out how we're going to answer these Hessians, first of all, and then we have to think about what we're going to do about General Washington. Though what are we going to do about that—go back in time?

Again?

Then we hear a scream. From behind us.

Bev.

NINE

BEV SCREAMS FIRST, THEN says: "Get away from me, you stupid Hessian!"

So that tells us something.

That tells us those guys had no intention whatsoever of *surrendering*.

That they thought we were just a bunch of stupid *kids*.

Brandon plows through the snow to where Bev is screaming.

I follow. I have an iPhone, which I hold aloft, like it's a weapon, but you know what?

It's not.

Not even pictures are going to help.

Brandon gets there first, and I'm right behind. To the edge of the woods, where Bev has gone to go.

The other dude dressed as a farmer has Bev. He has a hand over her mouth, and then he just lifts her up and takes off, like she's a giant loaf of bread.

Then we hear the English-speaking dude yell at Brandon and me. "Halt," he says. "Halt immediately! Or ve vill shoot to kill!"

"Easy, Brandon," I say, but Brandon isn't listening. I know I said that Brandon's not so dumb, but you know what?

Sometimes he is.

Like right now.

Maybe it's a New Mexico thing. Maybe in New Mexico they teach kids that snow has magic powers.

Brandon leans down, makes a giant snowball, and chucks it like it's a bomb that's going to do real damage somehow.

Mr. Butt-Ugly sees this and shouts something. I don't catch the word, exactly, but I'm pretty sure it's the German word for *Fire!*

Which they do.

We hit the deck. Or the snow, as is the case.

Nothing goes off at the same time. It's kind of a slow release kind of thing. *Bam,* we hear. Then not quite a *bam,* maybe some kind of misfire. That's it? One good shot, and one dud?

And we know what they have to do next: reload their muskets, which is not so easy a procedure. So we have time. Maybe thirty seconds.

Time enough to come up with a plan.

Which we might have done, if Brandon hadn't completely lost his cool.

He stands up, right there in the middle of the snow, and says something completely stupid.

I mean, really, really, really stupid.

Brandon says, "You want a piece of me? Huh? You want a piece of me? Well, here I come!"

He starts charging at them through the snow. His only weapons: snowballs.

I'm pretty certain he didn't think things through, but that's Brandon for you.

He's running, he's screaming, and then I hear a sick kind of *crunch*. Like what maybe a musket butt would sound like slamming into somebody's shoulder.

Then I hear thrashing and crashing, and a lot of foul words, most in English, some in German. Then another one of those sick *crunches*.

After that, a lot of rustling around. No arguments, though, and no English. Then a lot of footsteps crushing through snow, rushing away. The footsteps get fainter and fainter, until there's nothing but dead silence.

It's the silence that gets to me. That, and knowing our forces have now been reduced from three to one.

And I am the one.

TEN

I LET FIVE MINUTES GO BY.

Ten minutes.

I'm trying to think this through, I swear.

The situation has *deteriorated*.

It's gone from pretty bad to absolutely horrible.

Ten minutes turns into fifteen, and I'm beginning not to like snow so much. The stuff is everywhere. And I'm frozen to the bone.

Finally I decide to *do* something. A guy can sit around with his mouth agape for just so long.

I decide to *reconnoiter*.

Which is a word I've never, ever had a reason to use up until now.

I walk around and find a kind of ridge, and from here I can see the lay of the land.

We're on a farm. In the absolute middle of no-where. I can see the stable where George Washington is lying dead, I can see a couple of other small buildings we noticed before, and I can see a farmhouse, which is pretty much in the center of everything. The farm-house is made of stone, and it's not too big, nothing too fancy.

And that's where they all are.

All of them. Soldiers, fake farmers, and kids.

Everyone except me.

Alone, frozen solid, atop a hill. And in the nice warm farmhouse, my two other Left Behinds, two Hessians in full regalia, and two Hessians dressed like farmers.

I have to think this through all by myself.

I mean, we're talking big, big, big implications here, are we not?

Ummm, do you think George Washington being dead before crossing the Delaware River on Christmas night, 1776, counts as, you know, a *problem*?

Let's see: No Washington, no crossing. No cross-ing, no victory at Trenton for the troops. No victory at Trenton for the troops, no more army. No army, no revolution. No revolution, and everything we know—everything, but everything—doesn't go as it's supposed to go.

So that would be a problem.

And the thing is? I'm sitting here atop this hill, freez-ing my behind off, and I do not have a single, solitary clue what to do about any of it.

Not.
A.
Single.
Solitary.
Clue.

ELEVEN

THIS FARMHOUSE IS A little on the crooked side. It's kind of leaning right. Maybe they didn't plumb the thing when they built it. Smoke is pouring from a chimney. That must be the kitchen, probably the only warm place inside. I'd put the odds at one hundred percent that the kitchen is where everyone's gathered right about now.

I can get as close as I want, because they didn't bother to post a guard. Or as close as I dare, which are two different things. I want to peek in the window, see what there is to see.

I'm just not sure I dare to.

It's a *courage* thing, if you want to know the truth. Nobody would *see*, right? Nobody would *know* if I just sort of took a step back. A step or two back.

But when I hear someone whisper something right behind my left ear, I nearly jump out of my sneakers, and it's all I can do not to start wailing like a little bitty baby.

"Be still!" the voice says, a notch above a whisper. It's a girl's voice. "Hush!"

Another voice—a boy's, I think—then says, "We're not going to harm you. But don't thrash or they'll hear!"

I turn around. Two kids my own age, more or less, are behind me. One boy, one girl.

I'm betting they're related. Like, brother and sister. They both have freckles across the nose, brown eyes, and light brown hair, and they're dressed, unlike me, for the cold. Which means they have on long coats, boots, and hats. Well, the boy has on a hat—a tricornered job, naturally—and the girl has on a white bonnet, I guess is what they're called, tied under her chin. The boy puts his fingers to his lips. The girl puts her hands on her hips, and appears to be somewhat annoyed.

"Who are you?" I say.

"Who are *we*?" says the girl, incredulous. She has a funny kind of accent. Kind of English, and kind of not. Maybe about halfway between, which makes sense, if you think about it.

I do think about it, and that's when I realize: these two are natives. But not German. So there may be an upside here.

"Who are *we*?" the girl repeats. "It would be more

proper for us to ask you that. This is our property, after all. And you, sir, are trespassing."

"My name is Mel," I say.

"Mel?"

"Mel."

"Mel what?

"Just Mel."

"And where would you be from, Just Mel?"

"New Jersey. Basically."

"And is this," she says, looking me up and down, "how they dress in *New Jersey* these days? Whatever are those things on your feet?"

"Sister," the boy says. "Enough. We've been taught to welcome strangers, have we not? She's Elizabeth, I'm Daniel. Our parents own this farm, and that is our farmhouse, where you seem to be headed. We've been watching. Are you planning to surrender yourself?"

"Um, um," I say. "No, surrendering wasn't what I had in mind."

"Then what?" says the girl. "Were you planning a *rescue*?" She asks this as if it's the craziest thing she's ever heard of. "You haven't a single *weapon*, do you? These men are Hessians. Trained, professional soldiers. What were you planning to do—scare them by your mere presence?"

This might be 1776, but this girl—Elizabeth—would fit right in with the Kool Girl Gang in the Dining Hall at the Fredericksville School any old time. She's got the *sneer* part down pat.

I take out my iPhone and take her picture.

"This," I say, and turn the iPhone around to show her herself, "is my weapon. And I intend to use it."

TWELVE

B<small>UT SHE'S QUICK. Q</small>UICK to dismiss, quicker to sneer. "With this?" she says, glancing at her picture. "A *looking glass*? I grant you, those Hessians are ugly, for the most part. But unless your looking glass has musket balls, I'm afraid they won't be so easily scared off."

"It's not," I say, "a looking glass. It's an iPhone. It takes pictures, even movies. And plenty of other stuff."

"But is it a proper *weapon*?" asks the boy, Daniel. "Can it fire?"

"No," I concede. "It can't." But I'm really thinking, here we are, thirty yards from the farmhouse to which my fellow Fredericksville students have been abducted, separated one way or another by a gap of almost 240 years and, let's not forget, the Father of Our Country shot and killed in a horse stable a little ways away—and we're debating the *specs* of my iPhone?

The *capabilities* of the thing?

"So," says the girl, triumphant. "You have no weapons, then?"

"No," I say. "I guess I don't."

"And you weren't planning on surrendering?

"No, I was not."

"Then what were you planning on?"

"I was planning on . . . I was . . . I was just about to work something out. . . ."

"It seemed to us," she says, "that you were just about to run back the way you came. Which is the very reason we've had to intercede. You can't run, whoever you are. Do you not understand what is happening? The revolution itself is in grave danger. We've discovered their plans, which are to capture General Washington and kill him!"

I'm just about to say something snarky—*Oh, you don't say* was ready to roll off my tongue—when I think of something.

Now, we're standing in the snow. Like thirty, forty yards from the farmhouse.

Having a conversation.

Not making any particular effort to hide ourselves, either. Not that we could, because there's nothing around but snow. We could find trees or bushes or something else to hide behind, but then we wouldn't be thirty or forty yards away from the farmhouse. We'd be, like, a hundred yards away, or maybe two hundred.

Where we are is where you'd want to be if you were about to make a rescue attempt of some kind. It's not where you'd want to stand around and have any kind of extended conversation, which is exactly what we happen to be doing.

Because sooner or later, somebody in that farmhouse is going to notice.

Which is exactly what does happen. Some Hessian dude sticks his head out the door and shouts, *"Stoppen Sie sofort!"*

You'd be surprised by how fast kids can run in the snow, if properly motivated. Even if one of them is wearing sneakers.

I lead the way. It's their property, but I know where to go. We run full tilt all the way back to the horse stable.

No Hessian follows. For what, a bunch of kids? With Brandon and Bev they probably already have more than they want.

We get inside the stable, all panting and huffing, and it takes a minute to gather ourselves.

"Listen," I say. "I want to show you something. Don't get freaked or anything, all right?"

"Freaked?" says Daniel.

"Yeah. Don't get scared."

"Of what?"

"Let me show you." And I lead them to the stall, where General Washington lies dead.

He's whiter now than his hair.

The blood in the bullet hole in his chest has hardened. *Congealed*, I believe is the word.

"My Lord," says Elizabeth. Daniel takes off his hat.

Both of them fall to their knees and start to pray. Elizabeth, who as I said must be around my age, which is twelve and three months, starts to cry.

It takes them a few minutes. Which gives me plenty of time to realize that what I just did is kind of crummy.

To us, this whole thing has been like a weird dream, a funhouse adventure. But to Daniel and Elizabeth, this is *real*.

Daniel puts his arm around Elizabeth. She's rocking back and forth, holding her stomach as if she's racked with pain.

As if she's been stabbed in the gut.

"It's over," she says. "All of it. They'll hang the rest of them now, have their revenge. Father and Mother must be . . ."

Daniel puts his fingers to his lips, cutting her off. Then they both look up at me.

Tears in their eyes. Plus something new: fear.

We realize—all of us, at the exact same instant—that we don't trust each other.

THIRTEEN

M Y BRAIN—ACTING TOTALLY ON its own accord, believe me—sends an urgent message.

Get a weapon, it says. *Now!*

I'm pretty sure Daniel's brain and Elizabeth's brain
send them the same message. Because we all see the same
thing.

A pickax hanging on a wall. Opposite the stall where
General Washington lies dead.

The thing is, I have the advantage—I'm standing.
They're kneeling down. I'm clear-eyed, calm. They're dis-
traught and have tears in their eyes.

We all move for it at the same time.

With my right arm I do the most natural thing in the
world and give the nearest person a mighty stiff-arm. I
try for a face but get a chest instead.

Elizabeth's chest.

Which is not exactly, in this century or any other century, a gentlemanly thing to do.

She topples backward into Daniel, and they both tumble into the hay. Meanwhile, I grab the pickax with my left hand, swing it around, and turn.

The pickax is above my head, ready to come down, chop something up, or off.

Daniel and Elizabeth are on their backs, pure hatred flaring in their eyes.

"You fiend," Elizabeth hisses. "You absolute, horrible fiend. You shall burn in hell!"

She's not done. "You did this," she nearly yells. "You killed General Washington and then you brought us here to show off your handiwork. Murderer! Devil! You shall surely burn in hell!"

This is the second time today someone has called me a devil. First it was kind of fun. Now, not so much.

I put the pickax down. "Look," I say, "I didn't kill General Washington, and I'm not going to do anything to you. I need your help. These Germans have obviously done this and somehow commandeered your farmhouse. Right now they have my friends. None of us belong here. And I don't mean just here *here*. I mean we have to get out of this *century* and back to where we belong. But I don't think we can just yet. Because if George Washington dies now, before he crosses the Delaware, there may not be anything to return *to*. Nothing recognizable, anyway. So you see what I mean? We've got a big problem here. And like I said, I'm going to need your help."

I feel like I have just given a speech, but instead of applause, I get nothing but puzzled faces. Both Daniel and Elizabeth try, ever so slowly, to inch themselves backward in the stall.

"I think he may be a bit touched," whispers Daniel.

"By the devil, he is," answers Elizabeth.

"I'm not," I say. "I'm not touched, and I'm not crazy. But I need your help. First thing we have to do is help my friends."

"Why," Daniel says, "do you have to get out of this century? What is the meaning of this? And where exactly do you belong?"

"It's a long story," I say. "And I don't think you'd ever believe me. I don't think I even believe it myself."

"And you ask us to help you?" Elizabeth says. "Why ever should we? You trespass upon our property, you show us a magical box, and then you bring us to see the body of General Washington. Then you say your desire is to leave this century. And ask our help in so doing! So that you and your friends shall be gone with your box of magic, and we remain here? With a murdered General Washington in our horse stable? Who, think you, shall be blamed?"

"Our father," Daniel says. "Firstly. Which means we shall always have the mark upon us. As the family that betrayed the revolution, and brought General Washington to his end."

I slump down to the floor of the stable so I'm at eye level with both of them. Elizabeth has tears in her eyes, and Daniel isn't far off from having tears himself.

Neither am I.

"We don't belong here," I say. "My friends and me. We're just kids. Like you. One minute we're doing one thing, and the next—boom, we're right here in this stable. And it's all a gigantic mistake. That's the one thing I'm sure of. None of this is *supposed* to be happening. Not one part of it. General Washington can't be killed here, he just *can't* be. Do you see what I'm saying? If we let it happen, everything will go wrong—everything!"

"You speak," Daniel says, "as if we still have some say in the matter. As if a death is not final."

I take my iPhone out of my pocket. "This," I say, "is the key. Whatever happened, it has something to do with this."

"Your magical box?" says Elizabeth. "That you pretended was a weapon?"

"You're right, it's not a weapon," I say. "It's a phone. An iPhone, to be exact. Where I come from everybody has one, or something similar. And you want to know how come I'm so sure it's the key to all this? Why I'm one hundred percent certain?"

They stare at me, then at the phone. "Tell us then," says Daniel.

"Because it's the year 1776, right?"

"It is," says Elizabeth. "It can be no other."

"Okay, so tell me how somebody can send a text, then. In 1776. Because our teacher, Mr. Hart, has sent me, like, five texts. Explain that to me."

"A text?" says Daniel. "Do you mean, as in a book? Like the Bible?"

I stand up now because I'm starting to figure this out. "He texted me," I say. "He *texted* me. Do you understand what that means? It means all this . . ." I spread my arm, taking in the stable, the body of General Washington, the farmhouse. "All this isn't really real."

"It isn't?" says Daniel.

Elizabeth yanks on Daniel's coat and flits her eyebrows up and down. "He is touched," she says. "He speaks gibberish."

"I don't," I say. "What it means is that this isn't real. It *could* be real, if we don't do anything about it. Or it could be *changed*. I'm sure of it. Because if we could be here, that means we could be *anywhere*. Don't you see?"

"I'm afraid I do not," says Daniel. "I'm afraid I do not see a thing."

"You said you were worried about your father being blamed? About the mark your family would have on it for all time? Well, what I'm telling you is that we can do something about it. First off, let's go get my friends. Then, we'll change a little history. I think there's a way to make all of this right."

Elizabeth shakes her head and grabs hold of Daniel's coat.

"I'm going back," I say. "To the farmhouse." I lift up my pickax. "And I'm taking this. I hope you'll help."

"You shall go alone," Elizabeth says.

"Daniel? Are you sure?"

"Of you, I am not. Of my father being blamed, I am."

"Then you have a choice. You can either sit here and do nothing, like a potted plant, or you can come with me and do something."

I turn to go. If the "potted plant" crack works, I'll have to thank my dad.

FOURTEEN

A FEW MINUTES LATER I'M in front of the farmhouse, and I see everyone sitting down at a big table. Like they're waiting for dinner.

By *everyone*, I mean Bev and Brandon. They're sitting down. The Hessians, both uniformed and not, are standing up.

And dinner is not being served. iPhones are being served.

Both of them—one white, one black—are lying on the table. Then I notice something: I can't see any hands. Not a single one. Not Bev's, not Brandon's. No hands on the table, no hands scratching an ear or a nose, no hands nowhere.

They must have tied them behind their backs.

I'm outside the farmhouse, my feet in the snow, holding the pickax.

I now pretty much know the score. I know what kind of weapons they have, what kind of weapon I have.

I can do a lot of calculations, a lot of figuring, but I don't have a plan, exactly, just yet.

I'm thinking, I'm thinking.

Smash a window, throw in a fireball, burn the place down?

Make scary noises to cause half of them to run outside?

Wait until they all go to sleep?

I count off the Hessians: there's Mr. Butt-Ugly, the dude who speaks English; the other guy dressed in farmer clothes; and a soldier.

Three of them altogether.

Wait a second: weren't there four of them?

Where's Soldier Number Two?

A whole bunch of things happen all of a sudden.

I turn, I see him coming up behind me, and I swing my pickax with all I got.

I miss.

I miss him, that is. The farmhouse window? That I don't miss. I smash through, and while I'm at it I lose hold of the pickax. It flies through the window, glass shards spilling all over the place, and hits the very table where Bev and Brandon are sitting.

Everyone inside is, shall we say, *startled* a little. They

jump out of their boots, is what they do. But I only get to watch their reaction for maybe like a nanosecond, because Soldier Number Two, who I tried to whack with the pickax, doesn't seem startled at all. In fact, he seems kind of angry, if I had to put a word to it. Plus, he has a musket, with a big, sharp bayonet at its end. And he rears back, like he has every intention of ramming the thing straight through me.

Inside the farmhouse, I hear Brandon say something, and I hear Bev shout something too. I'd love to know more about what's going on, but there's this thrusting bayonet, you see, coming at me.

I duck.

I hit the deck.

He misses.

Then he recoils, tries again.

The *deck*, by the way, the so-called *deck*, is nothing but snow. His second swipe lands a micrometer from my neck. I twist, he strikes snow.

Then his legs are pulled out from under him. He falls, falls, falls and his musket goes up, up, up.

More shouts, screams from inside. Something crashing, something banging. English words, German words.

Daniel and Elizabeth run across my field of vision, Daniel holding on to a long length of thick rope.

Now the musket is coming down, down, down. I get to my feet, reach for it, reach for it, get it.

I swing around.

I point it through the smashed window.

I see Mr. Butt-Ugly standing over Brandon, arm raised, a pistol in his hand.

For a second I think I hallucinate.

I think I see something very odd. The pistol in Butt-Ugly's hand? Is it a German Luger, circa World War II? Which is not possible, as the thing surely hasn't been invented yet.

But whatever. The advantage is mine. I point the musket through the window. It's a heavy thing, this musket, and really long—like, about three-quarters as tall as me, practically. I can tell right away I won't be able to hold the thing straight out for very long—I'm not strong enough. I'm also wondering if it's loaded, if you just have to pull the trigger, or do you have to cock it first, or what? I ought to be able to do it because I saw a musket-firing demo at the reenactment.

I squeeze the trigger and nothing happens.

Then I cock it. Which means I pull this thingamajig back until it clicks into place.

Then I squeeze it again.

FIFTEEN

HAD THE THING BEEN loaded, it would have fired. Had my aim been true, ol' Butt-Ugly would have gotten plugged in the head, which might have ended the whole thing there and then.

Might have.

Doesn't.

Butt-Ugly is really ticked off. He's holding this pistol, remember, which really *does* appear to be a Luger. He yanks the pickax from the table and flings it back at me.

Fast.

It flies through the window.

I duck, I hit the deck, round two.

The pickax sails above my head, lands in the snow.

Soldier Number Two gets to it before I do. He's also ticked off about having his legs yanked out from under him. About losing his musket to a kid. About having to be the guy marching around in the snow while everyone else gets to warm up inside.

So he grabs the pickax, raises it above his head with both arms, and is just about to bring it down. But he forgets one thing. One very important item.

I still have his musket.

He starts to swing the pickax, and I do what anyone in my sneakers would do.

I stick him in the belly with his musket.

Hard.

It's lucky for him it's the butt end, not the business end, of the musket.

He goes, *Arrrrrrr.*

Arrrrrrr, like a pirate.

His arms were above his head, his big fat belly was totally exposed, and I hit him as hard as I could.

That's when he went, *Arrrrrrr.*

The guy staggers backward.

Bev screams: "Mel!"

Butt-Ugly raises his Luger. Hallucination or not, I'm calling 'em like I see 'em, and I say it *is* a Luger.

He fires.

His Luger, unlike my rifle, is loaded and ready.

It goes: *boom.*

SIXTEEN

DON'T DODGE BULLETS.

In case you're wondering.

I don't dodge bullets, I don't leap tall buildings in a single bound, and, normally speaking, I don't fight for truth, justice, and the American way.

I'm only twelve years old, for crying out loud. Well, twelve years and three months, if you want to be technical.

So when a guy points a pistol at me and fires, what do you expect me to do about it?

If you guessed not much, you guessed right.

Butt-Ugly fires; I stare. That's pretty much it. I see a little burst of yellow fire shoot out of his pistol, I hear the *boom* of the shot, but I don't really do much of anything else. I don't feint left, dodge right. I don't hit the deck. I just stand there, staring, and I don't even have much time to think things through. To think: *Oh, this must be the last second of my life. What* were *all those things I was going to do? Or: I'm so sad. How I'll miss my dear old dad and mom.* My life—all twelve years and three months of it—does not flash before my very eyes.

I kind of fritz out, if you want to know the truth of it. I *freeze.* My mind goes like totally *blank.*

Boom.

You hear that, you wait for the next part, where things go bad.

Like, your life is over, in other words.

The end.

But I hear the *boom,* but no bang.

Boom, but no *bang.*

Meaning he missed from ten feet, or there was never a bullet in there in the first place.

Boom, no bang.

It takes me a long, long time—like two, three seconds—to process this.

He shoots, but I'm alive.

Then I see the other guys raise their muskets high. The one dressed as a farmer, and the one dressed as a soldier. Who, if I saw correctly out of the corner of my eye in one of the milliseconds just before Butt-Ugly raised his Luger, had been busy ramming rods down the barrels of their muskets. Which is how they load the things, remember. My data-processing center, otherwise known as my brain, sends out an alert.

A message.

Danger, it says.

Danger, danger, danger.

This time I don't just stand there, though. This time I hit the deck like a trained Navy Seal and scramble the heck away from the window.

Two shots blast right above my head: *boom* and *boom.*

I hear, at the same time, Daniel and Elizabeth, who are about thirty yards away from the firing line, but off to the side.

They're screaming. At the proverbial tops of their lungs. They're screaming *at* me. Or rather *to* me.

"Come!" they scream. "We have to get away!"

I'm so happy to hear the word *we.* It's nice, at a time like this, to feel included in things.

SEVENTEEN

THEN I HEAR BEV screaming too. From inside the farmhouse.

And you know what? I can't remember the last time two girls were screaming to me at the same time. Okay, I remember: like, never.

Bev screams: "Mel! Mel! Get away!" And her scream is cut off, like someone puts a hand over her mouth.

I'm scrambling away at this point, don't forget. Like a trained Navy Seal, or maybe like just an ordinary seal, the kind that has flippers instead of arms and legs. I'm scrambling through snow, my arms and hands and fingers and feet and toes are nearly frozen solid, but I'm making progress. I'm getting closer and closer to Daniel and Elizabeth, and if there's one main thing I'm thinking, it's this:

man, I'm glad these guys don't have automatic weapons. This whole gunpowder–ramrod musket thing is really helping me out, because it gives me a few extra precious seconds.

I get to Daniel and Elizabeth, who are hiding behind some kind of little stone thing. A well, I'm guessing.

Two more volleys fly above our heads.

Daniel grabs my arm: "We have to get out of here. They're armed, we're not. It's hopeless if we stay and fight."

"What about my friends?" I say.

"You can't help them," Elizabeth says. "They told you so themselves."

When was it—all of ten, fifteen minutes ago—when we were in the horse stable and just about ready to kill each other? Things can change in a hurry if the muskets start going. "What made you come?" I say.

"If there's any chance," says Elizabeth. "Any chance at all . . . that our father will not be remembered . . . that General Washington will not be . . . we decided it was better . . ."

"To try," says Daniel. "Instead of try not. Now, we must go. Follow us. We know where to hide, so they'll never find us."

We move out. Zigging and zagging. About seven minutes later we're on another small hill, and we glance back: no soldiers. They've decided to stay put. A Bev and a Brandon and two iPhones, it appears, are more important than us.

I have to take a break. I'm panting, I'm huffing, I'm puffing, I'm sweating like a pig, and I'm frozen to the bone.

I sit down in the snow and take out my iPhone. And you know what? At this point I don't really care what Daniel and Elizabeth think about it. They stare and frown, but they need to take a break as much as I do, so they sit.

One new text has come in.

From Mr. Hart, of course. He says: *What is your power situation? You need to have at least 50%.*

Really, Mr. Hart? And how is that going to help Bev and Brandon?

Why is that? I tap in.

It won't work with less than 50% power.

What exactly won't work?

Do you want to come back or don't you?

Of course. But we have a problem.

What?

Bev and Brandon have been kind of captured.

Hessians?

Yes.

Armed?

Yes.

You?

No.

There's a pause. I take advantage: *Plus can't get more power—no electricity here.*

No response. I'm down to five percent power, but I'm beginning to think it doesn't matter, especially if there's nothing to be done about it. Also, why fifty percent? What does Mr. Hart know, anyway? And what isn't he saying? I tap in: *Mr. Hart, what's going on? Why are we HERE?*

It's a while before I hear the three-chord mini melody. I read: *How much power now?*

5 percent, I answer back. And notice he didn't answer my question.

Then this: *Turn off! Urgent you conserve power!*

I turn off my phone. Meanwhile, Daniel and Elizabeth stand up. They want to get moving, but I have a new idea. One that might be able to help us all out, General Washington included.

It's totally crazy. Yet I'm sure it's right.

"Is there any way," I ask, "that you could get me to Philadelphia?"

"Philadelphia?" Elizabeth asks. "Whatever in the world for?"

"I need to see someone," I say. "He might be our only hope."

"And who would that be?" Daniel asks.

"Dr. Benjamin Franklin," I say. "Who else?"

DR. FRANKLIN'S PHILADELPHIA

EIGHTEEN

I MIGHT AS WELL HAVE asked if they wouldn't mind giving me a lift to the moon.

"Philadelphia?" says Elizabeth. "It is miles away. I don't see how . . . I don't think it would be possible . . ."

"It's only, what, thirty miles from here?" I say. "Thirty-five, max. How long would it take us—an hour or two?"

"Are you proposing that you walk?" Daniel says. "In this weather?"

"No. I'm proposing we get there the fastest way possible. So I can see Dr. Franklin. And he can do something for me. Which if it works will solve everyone's problems."

"What is it you want him to do?"

I hold out my iPhone. "Fix this," I say.

"What's wrong with it?" says Elizabeth.

"It broke," I say. "And it needs to be fixed. I believe Benjamin Franklin is the only man alive who can fix it."

I'm not getting the sense that they're mildly reluctant to help. I'm getting the sense that they will absolutely refuse to help me under any circumstances whatsoever.

Which won't be good.

Because there's no way I'll be able to get from here to there without their help.

"Look," I say. "It's cold. It's hard to think. Is there someplace warm we can go to talk this over?"

Neither makes a move.

"It won't go away," I say. "The *problem*. Not by itself, it won't."

"The problem?" says Elizabeth.

"The problem. That would be General George Washington. Who just happens to be lying dead as a post in your father's horse stable. Have you guys thought this through?"

They obviously haven't, so I spell it out for them. "Okay, here's what's going to happen. At some point— probably soon—Washington's men are going to wonder where he is. They'll start to look for him, if they haven't already. They'll find him in your barn. No matter what excuse your father tries to come up with, it's *his* farm and *his* barn. How do you think this is going to go over? With Washington's men, for starters?"

"Perhaps not so well," Daniel says.

"Yeah. Perhaps not. Perhaps real badly. Put it this way:

I wouldn't want to be in your father's shoes. Not when a few thousand soldiers find out their leader has been killed on his property."

"But he didn't do anything!" Elizabeth says without conviction. "He wouldn't . . . he is not . . ."

"He's right, sister," says Daniel. "I fear Father knows not what he has done. Perhaps it would be better if we could find someplace warm to talk."

Then he starts walking. Elizabeth follows him, and I follow her.

We go along a pathway that connects to a sort of road. It's a little hard to tell what's what with all the snow, but Daniel and Elizabeth know the way. Up the road a bit we come to a small stone house, this one right by the road, not set back from it. It's where they're staying, Elizabeth tells me. Daniel, Elizabeth, their mother and father, and their six other brothers and sisters. The house belongs to an uncle, who has his own brood of older kids, but no wife. She died the year before. Of exhaustion, Elizabeth tells me. And unhappiness.

"'Twas not the cause," says Daniel. "'Twas a disease. Doctor said. I've forgotten which one, though."

"All right," Elizabeth says. "Have it your way. She was so exhausted and so unhappy she caught herself a disease. The same result in the end, isn't it?"

"My sister is not pleased," Daniel tells me, "on account of all of us having to live with . . . live here."

"With *him*," Elizabeth says. "Our dear uncle James. A

loathsome man if ever there was one. He thinks me his maid." Her eyes flare.

"Did the Hessians force you out?" I ask.

"Oh no," says Elizabeth. "They paid Father for the privilege. Most handsomely, I might add. Our dear uncle has staked a claim to half, on account of his putting us up for the fortnight.

"And now we know what they were up to. The pretense was that they were farmers, simple folk, German, of course, but simple. Not entwined in the revolution, not soldiers. Father allowed himself to be convinced. Mother was not, nor were we. But Father saw the gold and took it. We heard him tell Mother it was more than he could make in a year and a half."

We walk past the stone house, come to a barn, set back maybe thirty yards from the road. "Uncle is not a farmer," Daniel says. "He's a tradesman."

"What's his trade?" I ask.

"Furs," Daniel says. "Mostly."

"Whiskey," Elizabeth says. "And muskets. In return for furs. He takes trips, Uncle James does. To Western country. Once a month. Stays two weeks. Always comes back in a foul mood. And in a foul odor."

"Elizabeth," says Daniel.

"'Tis true, brother," she says. "And well you know it."

Daniel opens the door to the barn, and there before us, as if sitting in a place of honor, is a carriage. Uncle's carriage, no doubt.

I know nothing about carriages, or buggies, or whatever you call them, but this thing? It's old, decrepit, beat up, and smelly.

It's got two wheels, a torn-to-bits black cover made of some kind of fabric, a bench to sit on, and, projecting frontward, two long wooden shafts, which I suppose latch on to a horse somehow. The shafts aren't hooked up to anything at the moment, though. They're resting on the ground, so the whole contraption leans forward, like it's just about ready to fall apart.

"Hey," I say, and I try to force up some enthusiasm, like it's a brand-new Ford F-150 pickup. "Maybe we could take this?"

"Uncle's shay?" Daniel says.

"Shay? Is that what this is called?"

"Yes. But no one else is allowed to use it. Although he won't need it until next week."

"Daniel," says Elizabeth. "Have you thought of Uncle's reaction?"

"I have, sister. He'll be quite furious about it, but if we leave first thing in the morning, he won't be able to catch us."

NINETEEN

I WIND UP SPENDING THE night in the barn. And we leave pretty much at first light.

Sounds simple, doesn't it? Spend the night, then leave.

I'm not mentioning the fact that I had to spend about an hour and a half explaining myself to Daniel and Elizabeth. They wanted to know *everything*.

I said: You mean, like you want to know the *truth*?

Of course, they said: What else?

So I told them.

It wasn't my story that they believed. It was my clothes—I'm still wearing jeans, a jacket, white Nikes—and my iPhone.

I let them hold it. I turned it on for a few seconds so they could tap some icons. Daniel couldn't get over the calculator, and kept putting in numbers. "If only we could use this at market," he said. "The buyers always seem to miscalculate in their own favor, and Father never comes home with what he thinks he should have been paid."

And I won't mention that later, they came back in with some food—a hunk of ham and a chunk of bread. Or that I had to sleep in a bed of hay and froze my butt off. Or that I couldn't help asking myself questions.

Terrible questions that had no answers.

Like: how did all this happen, anyway? Why are we *here*?

Are Bev and Brandon going to be all right?

What about our *parents*? Brandon's mom, Bev's mom, my mom and dad—wouldn't they be a little bit *concerned* by now?

Do they even know we aren't at school?

And let's not forget: What is the *deal* with General Washington? Is he really, you know, *dead* dead? And if so, what the heck does it all *mean*?

Finally, when Daniel and Elizabeth left for the night, I thought they believed me, and I thought I could trust them. That the plan we had come up with—we'd take Uncle James's one-horse shay all the way to Philadelphia, find Dr. Franklin, somehow get everything *fixed*—was a good one.

It won't surprise you that I got, like, no sleep. Even if I'd had nothing on my mind, it still would have been freezing. And what if Daniel and Elizabeth changed sides and decided to tell their father and their uncle there was this super-weird kid who claimed he was from the future sleeping in the barn? What if in the morning they'd find a sheriff or a constable or whatever they called the local law-enforcement dude and turn me in?

Which, even if they did, wouldn't *solve* anything. A constable wouldn't make General Washington *undead*. Wouldn't do a thing for Bev or Brandon.

At dawn, Daniel and Elizabeth quietly come into the barn. Elizabeth brings me breakfast—a biscuit, another piece of ham—while Daniel gets their uncle James's shay prepared. "We've told Father and Mother," Elizabeth says, "that we will be visiting our grandmother. Who lives in Doylestown. And they have prevailed upon Uncle James to lend us his shay. But instead of west to Doylestown, we will go south to Philadelphia."

"Juniper will take us," Daniel says. "Juniper knows the way."

"Juniper?" I ask.

"Juniper," says Elizabeth. "Uncle James's favorite mare."

And then we're off.

But Juniper is in no hurry. Turns out she came with only two gears—slow and slower. After the first hour, Philadelphia seems far, far away.

TWENTY

B ELIEVE IT OR NOT, there are roads.
Sort of.

Nothing like I'm used to. No signs, no traffic lights, no pavement, no lines in the middle, no shoulders, no fast lanes, no rest stops, no eighteen-wheelers, no highway patrol, no talk radio to help while away the time.

But a road nonetheless. With ruts through the snow, made by hearty fellow travelers who've gone before us. This is 1776, keep in mind; the folks around these parts know how to *deal*.

So, once we get to the road, it's not so hard to stay on the road. You just keep going, in the direction you're pointing to. And then it's nothing but *cloppity-cloppity-cloppity-clop*.

It's about thirty miles to Philadelphia. In good weather, a one-horse shay like Uncle James's goes about four or five miles an hour. In bad weather, or in snow, we're talking about two or three miles an hour. Meaning, it's going to take ten to fifteen hours to get to Philadelphia.

That's a long time to be sitting on a plank of wood in the cold, without anything to plug in, watch, or read.

We talk. They want to know everything they possibly can about my world, and I want to know everything about theirs. They both were taught to read by their mother. For a time, they both attended a sort of school—a tutor gave separate lessons to boys and girls—but the tutor moved on as the war took hold, apparently to go west where there was less fighting. Elizabeth didn't take to school as well as Daniel, who still has hopes that one day the tutor might return. Otherwise, it'll be farming for him, and marriage for Elizabeth.

We take turns driving. I've never driven a one-horse shay before, but it doesn't take long to get the hang of it. You basically just sit there, hold the reins, and let the horse do the work. Juniper knows the route.

By four o'clock in the afternoon, we've all had enough. Especially Juniper, who's been doing all the work. The problem is, we're only a little more than halfway there.

We stop at an inn. There's a stable for Juniper to spend the night in, food for us to eat, and rooms for us to sleep in.

"Father knows the owner," Elizabeth says. "And his

credit is good. We'll have to explain when the bill comes due, as this is not on the way to Doylestown."

"I'll pay you back," I say. But I don't say how, because the truth is I don't think there's any way I ever could.

The innkeeper is a gruff man of few words, but he does know Daniel and Elizabeth's father, and he lets us stay. The inn has everything we need: food for us, a warm stable for Juniper, and a single room with two beds—one for me, one for Daniel and Elizabeth. The only problem is the "necessary."

The bathroom, in other words. It's behind the inn. Ye olde outhouse.

Put it this way: the fact that it's freezing cold is not the worst thing about this particular "necessary." Not by a long shot.

At least Bev isn't around. She'd go into major snit mode and nobody would get any sleep.

TWENTY-ONE

I T'S AROUND TWO IN the afternoon when we enter Philadelphia. I can tell right away we're in a city, because the place is, like, super stinky.

Horses. They got to do what they got to do, which unfortunately is all over the street. Which happens to be sort of covered with snow. So what the horses do is all too clear to see, let alone smell.

To call this a city is a stretch. There are houses, small buildings, and more roads than just the one we came in on. There are other carriages besides ours, and there are plenty of people—all bundled up—going in and out of places. We are on Market Street; there are stores and shops all over, so to market everyone goes. It's two days after Christmas now, remember. People are busy, got to get their stuff, just like in our day. No one pays us any mind, though. We chug halfway up Market before we think to ask anyone where to go.

Daniel calls out to the first passerby we come across. He's a man, a merchant perhaps, and maybe a Quaker. He's wearing one of those hats—black, wide-brimmed, upright.

"Good sir," says Daniel. "We are seeking a certain personage, a resident of Philadelphia. Our business is most important."

The man stops, regards us closely, approaches our shay. "Perhaps I can help. Who is this personage you speak of?"

"Dr. Franklin," says Daniel.

"Dr. Franklin?" he says. "Benjamin Franklin?"

"The very one, sir," says Daniel. "Would you be kind enough to direct us to his place of residence?"

"I certainly could, if he were here—everyone knows the residence of Philadelphia's most celebrated personage, as you put it. But I believe the esteemed Dr. Franklin has left. He should be back soon enough, young man. Six months to a year, I reckon."

"Six months to a year?"

"He has accepted an assignment, from what the gazettes say. To be the representative to the king of France."

"The king of France?"

"Yes, indeed. You see what happens, young man, when you go about and start a rebellion and declare independence? Then you are required to send an emissary to the king of France. Franklin was chosen. I believe he left last month. Good day to you!"

TWENTY-TWO

WE DON'T HAVE LONG to be astounded. The man walks off, but we get ourselves a bit of attention. Two, three, four, five other folks have paused in their comings and goings to listen to our conversation. Most then go about their business; one does not.

She's an older lady, and she's lost most of her teeth. She has some kind of frayed bonnet on her head, and she walks with a bit of a stoop. She also keeps shifting her eyes to the left, then to the right, then to the left again, as if she has a secret, or something to hide.

"It's not what I've been hearing," she says, eyes left, eyes right. "Not what I've been hearing at all."

She's standing next to the shay. As if she knows something.

"Is that so?" I say.

"That is so," she says.

"What are you hearing?"

"I'm hearing something quite different," she says. "Something quite different indeed. But I've encountered some difficulties as of late. A small consideration . . ."

I don't have my wallet with me, but in my pants' pocket I have a five and three ones I'd brought to the reenactment in case I wanted to buy something, like a souvenir knickknack or a can of Coke.

I first show the five and the ones to Daniel and Elizabeth.

They're intrigued. As far as Elizabeth is concerned, a one-dollar bill beats an iPhone.

"My word," she says. "There he is. General Washington."

"Yes," I say, and show one to the old woman. Her eyes go wide.

"See this?" I say. "It's the new currency. General Washington himself is on this bill. And guarantees its value one hundred percent."

She reaches for it. She wants it more than she's wanted anything in her life, but I pull it away. "First, I need to hear what you've been hearing. If it's of value, the bill is yours."

She steps forward. She's a bit of a mangled old lady—her hair is white and stringy, she has spots on her face, and she smells almost as bad as the horses. Her eyes shift left, then right, then left again. "I hear," she says in a whisper, "that Dr. Franklin never made his ship to France. That he was, shall we say, a bit indisposed at the time of departure. And not alone, if you understand my meaning. But so mortified is he about missing the departure that he's lying low, awaiting the next ship."

"Lying low? Lying low where?"

She smiles her toothless smile. "For that, I would need special consideration."

I wave two dollar bills before her. "They're yours," I say. "Two. But only for the truth."

"Near the end of Market," she says. "One of the buildings he owns. No tenants, so there he stays, till he finds a ship that sails. And prays no one discovers him!"

She grabs the ones and is off. And so are we, to near the very end of Market Street.

TWENTY-THREE

A FEW MINUTES LATER WE come to a small, tidy
building. There's no one in the street, thankfully.
It's gotten colder, by the way, and the wind has picked up.
Our poor horse, Juniper, has probably done as much as
she is able, and needs to rest. We tie her up, and get out.
There's no number on the door, and no marking. I lift my
hand and rap, two sharps and one flat.

Nothing.

I try again, louder, more insistent. *Rap, rap. Rap, rap.
Rap.*

Something stirs.

Rap rap rap rap rap.

Someone sighs.

Rap rap rap.

"Shush!" someone says. The voice is a man's voice, a man of a certain age: not so young. Not at all young. He shouts a single shush, nothing more.

We wait.

We wait some more.

The temperature drops, the wind increases, and poor Juniper snorts like she's saying, *What about me?*

I rap again. Three hard ones. *Rap. Rap. Rap.*

No sound, but a slight lifting of a lace curtain covering a side window. And, peering through, a man in spectacles.

Bald up top, long gray hair behind.

An unmistakable man. Dr. Benjamin Franklin himself.

He's positively *glowering* at us. I can think of only one thing that might take the steam off—I take out my iPhone and wave it in front of the window. The eyes widen at once, and we hear a shuffling to the door. Then we hear keys, latches, locks. Something is undone, or unlocked, and the door opens a crack.

A hand extends. A single hand, a left one. No rings. But crusty-ish, the hand of an older man, with yellowed nails and spots. The hand makes a gesture, a gesture recognizable today, or in 1776, or probably as long as humans have had hands. The gesture is an impatient double flick of the fingers. It means one thing, in any language: gimme.

Fork it over.

I fork it over. I lay the iPhone on the open palm of Dr. Ben Franklin. His hand encircles it, fondles it almost, then immediately slithers back inside the door.

The door shuts.

"Hey!" I shout. "That's mine! Give it back!"

Silence. Then another peek from behind the curtain.

"Give it back!" I say again.

"I quite like this," he says, from behind the door. "It does intrigue me. I would like to know its function, but first, may I have it?"

"You may not," I say, and raise my hand to the window, and give him the same gesture he had given me: fork it back.

He opens the door, and into my outstretched palm he places something round and brown. "Here you are," he says.

"What's this?"

"A twopence."

"A twopence?"

"A twopence!" he shouts, and slams the door and locks it. "Now good day to you, young man! Be off!"

TWENTY-FOUR

Have you ever seen a twopence? He called it "tuh-pence," by the way, not "two-pence." I have no idea what a twopence could get you in Dr. Franklin's Philadelphia, but I doubt it could be much more than half a loaf of bread. A twopence, for an iPhone? You've got to be kidding me.

Rap, rap, rappy rap rap rap. "Hey!" I shout. I rattle the doorknob, and kick the bottom of the door while I'm at it. Dr. Franklin may not be aware of this, but he is certainly about to learn: no one messes with a twelve-year-old and his iPhone. I mean no one, not even a world historical figure. Not even the guy who invented electricity.

"Hey!" I shout. "Open up the door, will ya?"

"Be kind, Mel," Daniel says. "A stir shan't be of help to anyone."

"But he has my phone! He just . . . he just . . . he just took the thing! What a jerk!"

Elizabeth takes offense. "You are referring to Dr. Benjamin Franklin. He is our most esteemed scientist and philosopher. Who also signed the Declaration of Independence. Which means he has put his life on the line— he'll be hanged along with the rest of them if the British should prevail. So I think your choice of words ought to be more respectful, if you please."

"But he took my phone! Which happens to be the reason we came here in the first place."

"To have your phone taken?" she asks.

"To have my phone *examined*," I say. "Because I think it's the thing that brought us here. Somehow or other." I give five more knocks on the door by way of exclamation. And, at the bottom, one solid kick.

We have, by now, attracted some interest from people in the street. And I remember that Dr. Franklin isn't in this house near the end of Market Street by *accident*. The old lady had told us that he was . . . *hiding out*. I have a hunch that the good doctor does not want to be *seen* by anyone. So the longer I stay here knocking and kicking on his door, the worse it'll get for him.

Advantage: Mel.

"I'm not going away," I say, through the door. I try to modulate my voice so that only he can hear me. "And a certain amount of attention has been generated. People want to know what's going on. At the house at the end of Market Street. Your best course, sir, is to let us in. Forthwith."

I think it was the *forthwith* that got to him. A pretty fancy word, isn't it? I didn't even know I knew it. Certainly I had never said it aloud to anyone before. But either that or something else did the trick, because we hear shuffling again, unlatching again, and then the door swings open.

TWENTY-FIVE

Dr. Ben Franklin stands before us. He's definitely old, and he's definitely . . . stout. "Well?" he says.

"We want to come in," I say. "And talk."

"Talk?"

"Yes. Five minutes is all we ask."

He notices my Nikes. "Whatever are those things on your feet?"

"They're called *sneakers*," I say.

"Sneakers?"

"Yes."

"I have never heard of or seen such things. Are they made in a shoemaker's? Have they . . . some useful function?"

I knew these Nikes were going to be a problem.

Elizabeth steps in to help. "We have more urgent business, sir," she says, "than what our friend wears upon his feet."

Dr. Franklin shakes his head, then steps aside. "Five minutes," he says. "And hurry before you let the cold in." He waves us inside, closes the door, and peers through the window, to see, presumably, what kind of commotion we stirred up.

The house is very small, the hallways are very narrow, and the ceiling is very low. We stand in the foyer. Now that we're in the actual presence of the Great Man, we have all, collectively and simultaneously, lost our tongues.

"Come now," he says, and leads us down a hall to a sitting room. The floors are very creaky. Dr. Franklin uses a cane, and his right foot drags somewhat, as if he can't put weight on it. He motions at some stiff wooden chairs for us to sit on. Then, with a great deal of show and effort, he plops himself down on a very small cushioned armchair, which sinks with the weight of him. He lays his cane down, adjusts his spectacles, and then opens his palm. My iPhone.

"So then," he says. "Who have we here? And why have you come?"

Daniel, being properly of the time and place, takes the lead. "We—my sister and I—come from upriver. Thirty miles north, where my parents have a farm. A pair of strange German men, dressed as ordinary farmers, have bargained with my father for the use of his farm for a short while. 'Twas there we met our new friend here," Daniel says, and nods at me. "He's not from these parts. Not exactly, that is."

"And, sir," says Elizabeth, "worst of all? General Washington has been murdered. We saw his body. By the very same Germans my brother spoke of."

"Oh my dear Lord," Dr. Franklin says. "Oh my good dear Lord." Then he lurches forward involuntarily, as if someone has just socked him in the gut.

Which someone has.

We give him a moment and watch, helpless, as the old man winces, and rocks, and then heaves. "Oh my good dear Lord," he says again. "What will ever happen to us now? We shall have no army. Only Washington could gather them. Only Washington could lead them. And only Washington could get them to fight. We are sunk without him. My God. I never thought it would happen. Never for a second did I harbor any doubt whatsoever. I was sure, sure in my bones, that we were favored by the Almighty. That independence was our destiny."

"It was," I say. "And it is. That's what we've come to talk to you about."

Dr. Franklin blinks. Then he waves his hand. "About our destiny? About independence? But now all is for naught. If Washington is dead, I am quite certain our revolution is defeated."

"Dr. Franklin," I say, "let me give this to you straight. I am of a different time. The twenty-first century, to be exact. And there has been some mistake: General Washington was not supposed to die. In fact, he *cannot* die. The future of the whole world depends upon it. We've come to you to help us figure out a way to *undo* what's been done. And I'm pretty sure the key to it is sitting right there in your hand. It's called an iPhone."

Dr. Franklin looks down, sees the thing in his hand, and drops it on the floor, like it's the hottest potato in history.

TWENTY-SIX

"**H**EY, MAN!" I SAY. "Easy!" Then I reach down and pick up my phone, which feels good back in my hands: *my precious, my precious!*

And I don't mean to be rude or anything, especially not to one of America's Founding Fathers, but the floor is made of wood, you know? He could have broken it, and then where would we be? I do a quick inspection; luckily everything still works and the glass didn't break.

"Dr. Franklin," I say. "We've come to you for help. This device?" I hold up the phone. "It requires electricity, which you invented. We're hoping that there's some way you can provide it for us."

Dr. Franklin glances at Daniel and Elizabeth. "Is this so?" he asks them.

"It is," says Daniel. "Our only hope rests with you."

"Please listen to him, Dr. Franklin," says Elizabeth. "We have no other choice."

"Well," he says, leaning back in his chair. "I wouldn't say I *invented* electricity, exactly. It's been around since the dawn of earth, naturally, in the form of lightning, and many a court jester has been able to generate a charge of static electricity by the use of a long glass pipe, rubbed back and forth just so. But, to give myself what I hope is not undue credit, I would say that I was among the first to try to discern some of the physical properties of electricity. To properly understand what exactly its essence consists of, as it were. And I'm no theorist, mind you. A Sir Isaac Newton, with his formulas and equations, and his extraordinary explanations, in Latin, no less—well, suffice it to say, a Newton I am not. I am a practical man, an exceedingly practical man, if I say so myself, and therefore my interest in electricity is, and was, primarily to find a practical *purpose* for it. What could electricity be made to do? And, most important, could we find some feasible way . . . to *channel* its power . . . so its use could be for the betterment of mankind?"

We stare at him and say not a word.

"Ah," he says. "I see why you look at me so questioningly. Have I missed the essential point? It would not be for the first time, my dears. Because you, young man, are asking me for something. You are asking me to *provide* you electricity, not explain its properties. Forgive my digression. But what does this . . . this thing . . . have to do with the . . . killing of General Washington? I am having trouble indeed with this news you bring me. Firstly, I barely believe it, and require confirmation before I allow myself to plunge into the pits of despair. Secondly, you ask me to provide you electricity? At a time such as this? Whatever for?"

I can only think of one way to answer him. I turn on my phone and take a picture. Of Dr. Ben. Because, if you think about it, no one has ever taken this man's picture . . . ever.

Then I show him.

"By Jupiter," he says. "That is most amazing, young man. An astonishing trick. Tell me, how is it done? Is it a painting? An etching, perhaps? Have you had it prepared prior to your coming to see me?"

"It's not an etching or a painting, Dr. Franklin. It's what we call a *photograph*. Which is sort of . . . well, I guess you can call it an instant reproduction of something. And, among other things, this"—I hold up the iPhone—"can take thousands of them. Also, video, which is like a photograph, only moving." Then I point it at Dr. Franklin, at Elizabeth, and at Daniel, and shoot a little scene. Ten seconds.

Then I show them.

I'm down to four percent power, but it's now or never, I figure.

Daniel and Elizabeth are properly astonished at the

video clip. Dr. Franklin, alas, is not. Perhaps he doesn't like what he saw, or doesn't realize just how . . . old . . . and *stout* he really is.

"Young man," he says. "I demand that you give me that . . . that . . . whatever it is . . . this . . . object . . . immediately."

"I cannot, sir. Not until you agree to help us."

"Help you? I should say not. First you tell me General Washington is dead, then you ask me for electricity?"

"I haven't explained everything to you yet. You don't understand."

"Understand what? That you have some kind of clever . . . device . . . that you use in a wholly unjustified manner with no other purpose in mind than to horrify an old man?"

"I'm not trying to horrify you, Dr. Franklin. Like I said, we've come to you for help. Because something has gone terribly wrong."

"Yes, you told me. About General Washington. And that you yourself are from—from where did you say? The twenty-first century? How have I allowed myself to listen to such rank nonsense—and from *children*! I don't believe a word of it. Not a single word. I now must ask you to leave my premises. Immediately! And take that infernal device of yours with you! I wish to never see it for the rest of my days!"

TWENTY-SEVEN

A PICTURE, SO THEY SAY, is worth a thousand words. There's really nothing else for me to do, then, except turn the phone around, and show Dr. Franklin my Camera Roll.

I show him the pictures I took of Daniel and Elizabeth.

Then my other shots. From yesterday morning, in the van on the way over. A shot of Brandon with an inadvertent piece of cream cheese on his nose, from a bagel he had just wolfed down.

A shot of the crowd gathered at Washington Crossing State Park to watch the festivities. There's usually a fife and drum band, a speech by a politician or two, and then the ritual reenactment of Washington and his army crossing the Delaware in longboats.

Then I scroll around. I have a picture of my dad, and one of my mom. Not together, of course. They haven't been together since the divorce, and for quite some time before that as well.

Dr. Franklin coughs. A polite cough. To let me know something.

Which is, I've been staring at the picture of my mom.

And the whole point of this was to share, wasn't it?

"May I see?" Dr. Franklin asks, not unkindly. He holds his hand out.

I place the iPhone in his palm. He can see for himself how my mom is dressed. He begins to nod, as if something is starting to make sense. Daniel and Elizabeth gather behind Dr. Franklin, and, since I've showed them how my iPhone works, they take on the instructor's job.

"Press that," Daniel says. "It's called the home button." Dr. Franklin presses it with a very stubby forefinger.

My home screen. Messages, Calendar, App Store, Clock.

"Quite ingenious," says Dr. Franklin. "What is this device called again?"

"An iPhone," Elizabeth says quite proudly. It's almost as if she owns it herself.

"And its primary purpose?"

"It's a combination of things," I say, "but first and foremost, I guess, is that it's a phone."

"A phone?"

"A telephone. You can talk to someone else who has one. Anywhere in the world."

"Do you mean to say that I could . . . converse with someone . . . who is not in the same room as I?"

"Sure. You could have a live conversation with someone in a different city if you wanted, or even a different country."

"Hmmm. I am not so certain that is a good thing. You say 'live conversation,' which implies there is an opposite, namely, 'dead' conversation. Is your device capable of communicating with those no longer among us? I have heard of such things from those with a more mystical mind than mine."

"No. You can't talk to dead people with an iPhone. That would be crazy."

"I see," he says. "What provides its . . . its . . . energy?"

"A battery."

"A battery?"

"Yes. Built in."

"Remarkable. I daresay I did invent the battery, if not electricity. Most remarkable, young man. And how is it that . . . one can talk to another? Through what mechanism?"

"Um. I'm not quite sure of that. Sound waves? Alexander Graham Bell invented the telephone, but to tell you the truth I'm not sure how they work. This is wireless, though. Back in the old days, there was no such thing as wireless. Every phone had to have a cord to it. Which attached to the whole network, I guess."

"Network? What kind of network?"

"Well, again, I don't really know, exactly. I think a

network is where they keep all the cords and wires and stuff. And the routers, I think that has something to do with it. My dad put a router in at our house, but it never works right."

"A router? What is its purpose?" Then Dr. Franklin nods at Elizabeth, and points to a piece of paper and a pen he has nearby. Elizabeth brings him not only the pen, but an inkwell. As soon as the paper is in his hands he places a book in his lap and the paper upon it, and starts taking notes.

"Um . . . well, that's a good question."

"But you don't really know," he says, peering at me over his half-spectacles. I'm glad that he isn't my teacher, because if he were I'd be heading for an F.

"No. Not really. I just use it."

"Fair enough, young man. Let's return to these 'sound waves' you spoke of. What are they? Or do you not know?"

"Well, I do know something about that. Sounds are carried along, you see. On waves." I use my hand to show just how a wave goes. He follows my hand for a second before glancing at Daniel and Elizabeth and rolling his eyes.

"They are?"

"Yes."

"What sort of waves? Like in the ocean?"

"No. Invisible ones."

"Invisible waves?" says Elizabeth. "That surely must be quite impossible!"

"Well, it isn't. I learned about it in science class."

"Hmmm. A most interesting theory. Waves, you say? As in, the sound itself—say a clap of my hands—travels via an 'invisible wave' from source to ear?"

"Yes. Something like that."

"And this battery—you say it's 'built in'? Built into what—this device itself?"

"Yep."

"How could that be? It would have to be incredibly small."

"It is incredibly small. They figure out ways to make 'em that way. *Miniaturization* is what they call it."

"Miniaturization?"

"Yes."

"May I see it? This battery?"

"Well, no, you can't. Not with iPhones. Unless you unscrew it and mess things up."

"So what happens when the battery is drained of its charge? Is the device then useless?"

"No, because you can recharge the battery. I recharge mine every night, but if you use it a lot, you might lose power, which kind of stinks. As a matter of fact, I'm down to about three percent power right now. And I know we're going to need this phone. So problem number one is, do you think you could figure out a way to get some juice into this thing?"

He peers at me again, over the rim of his half-spectacles. "Juice," he says, frowning. "I shall take an intuitive leap, young man. You are not talking about the liquid that one can extract from a lemon, or a lime, or an apple. You are using this word 'juice' as a synonym, are you not? For electricity, yes?"

"Exactly," I say. He's an old dude, but he's one fast learner.

I'm not surprised. It's why we came to Philadelphia. He may not know it yet, but I am one hundred percent positive he's going to be able to help us. He's only Benjamin Franklin, after all, who happens to be the smartest guy in the world. He'll figure something out.

Won't he?

TWENTY-EIGHT

H E HANDS THE PHONE back. "Young man," he says. "I can't tell you how intrigued I am. I have a thousand questions more—two thousand. The most important of which is, of course, whatever has this . . . device . . . to do with General Washington? I am glad I have chosen not to believe what you have told me about his demise, for if I did—if it were true—I would be quite unable . . . quite unable to function, I fear. Do you know how we came to select Washington to lead us? It was mere months ago . . . perhaps a year . . . at the Second Continental Congress. A most deliberative body. Which is to say, there was very little all could agree on most of the time. But we had finally come to a decision: we should have ourselves an army. We cast our eyes about for someone to lead it, and who should walk into our ken but none other than the tallest man in the room, a man dressed—almost as if he were auditioning for the part—in full military regalia. A bit tight, to be sure, about the stomach and shoulders, but then I found out later the uniform was a relic from our good Virginian's youth. I turned at once to John Adams and said, 'There, sir, is our man.' And thus George Washington became General Washington."

Elizabeth gives me a nudge. "Get on with it," she says. "I suspect we haven't much time."

"Dr. Franklin," I say. "We really need your help. I mean, like right *now*, we do. The problem is, this device? If we don't do something soon, it will be totally useless."

"If you have come to me . . . with any expectation," Dr. Franklin says in a grave voice, "that I would be able to provide you some sort of practical assistance . . . such as regenerating this battery you speak of . . . then I'm afraid you're mistaken. I can provide you no help. To do what you ask, we would need to repair to my proper living quarters, or to one of my former businesses, where I at least have the necessary means and tools to examine the situation in a more efficacious manner. Here"—he gestures to the sitting room, the entire house we're in—"I am, quite unfortunately, utterly helpless. And here, also quite unfortunately, I must remain. I am in hiding, if you must know. I am officially incognito. Unofficially, I believe all of Philadelphia to know where I am and why I have delayed, but all of us must, for appearance's sake, play the game."

"You're in hiding from the British?"

"Oh good Lord, no. I am in hiding from my fellow countrymen, and, most particularly, my fellow revolutionaries. I have agreed, you see, to be our congress's representative to the king of France. And there I should be now, in the court of Louis the Sixteenth himself, had I sailed on the ship that was to bring me. It—the ship—sadly left without me, nearly a month ago now. I was detained at the time of the sailing. Unavoidably detained. I shall sail as soon as I am able and as soon as there is passage on an outbound ship, which I expect to occur within days. So here I am. And here shall I stay. And no help may I give you of a practical nature."

There's a silence as we all process what has just been said, and then a voice, from another room.

"Father," we hear. "Who are these children? And why . . ." She nods at us, sees that something about me isn't right. "And why are they here?"

A woman—thirty, maybe forty—enters our room via a doorway in the back. She is wearing a long dress. An apron. She has a bonnet, of sorts, a white frilly bonnet, on her head.

"We have come to save the revolution," Elizabeth says. "And only Dr. Franklin can help."

"My dear," the woman says. "I have heard those very words a dozen times, at the least. Why can only Dr. Franklin help this time?"

"Because," Elizabeth says, "General Washington is gone."

"Gone? Gone where?"

"To his grave," says Elizabeth. "He was white as a ghost. And quite dead. It was a blow to our hearts, to be sure. But he—Mel—has spun a tale so fantastical, he has given us hope."

"I see no hope," Dr. Franklin says, "if General Washington has perished. I will refuse to believe it until I must."

"The hope," I say, "is that in some way this death may be reversed."

"Reversed?" says Dr. Franklin. "How so? How may any death be 'reversed'? What alchemy is this?"

All eyes are upon me. So I say what's on my mind, and why not? It seems simple enough. "All we need to do," I say, "is figure out how I—and my friends—got to this century in the first place. Then we can reprogram things. So we arrive one hour earlier. When we can make sure nothing happens to General Washington."

"You see, Sally," says Dr. Franklin, "these children do not ask much. Only that I undo what has been done. If only I had that power—I could reorder all history!"

TWENTY-NINE

BEFORE ANYONE CAN REACT, there comes a knocking on the door.

"Dr. Franklin!" we hear someone shout. A man, who is trying to keep his voice down without much success.

"Dr. Franklin, I beseech you! I have urgent news! Of the utmost importance!"

Sally goes to the door, peers through the curtain. "It is Mr. Farrington," she says, "from the print shop. He seems agitated."

"Let him in, Sally," Dr. Franklin says. "By all means, let him in. Shall we not have a dinner dance, and let the whole of Philadelphia visit?"

"Now, Father," Sally says, and unlatches the door. Mr. Farrington enters. He is round, short, young, covered in snow, and red-faced.

"May I speak frankly, sir?" he says. "I have news of the utmost urgency."

"You may, Farrington, you may. We're all friends here. Tell me—by chance, does your news have to do with the revolution?"

"It does, sir."

"With a certain general who happens to command our army?"

"It does indeed, sir. A great, great tragedy—General Washington has been killed!"

"I did not want to believe it," Dr. Franklin says. "I prayed it was untrue. I still can scarce bring myself to accept it."

"But how could you know this, sir?" says Mr. Farrington. "This news was delivered to me not five minutes ago. I have been told to inform no one other than yourself. How could you possibly know already?"

Dr. Franklin nods at us. "These children," he says simply, "already knew. And told me."

"But the revolution, sir, the revolution! The soldiers are deserting by the score! They have raided the stores and are alighting upon the countryside! They are in a mad hunger, and they claim they have not been paid by Congress what they are owed and say that they intend to take whatever they can get in recompense!"

"So they likely shall," Dr. Franklin says, "for, sad to say, their lament is true. General Washington has warned us plain enough: the men must be paid. But the

Continental Congress has dithered, as usual. Dithered and discussed and dithered some more, as all assemblies of men are wont to do, and in the end decided nothing, did nothing. Of course, the Continental Congress has no money, no scrip, no tax-collecting authority, and therefore no means of generating revenue, save what our customs agents are able to procure. But trade has withered, hasn't it, since we proclaimed our independence? By day's end I fear we shall have no army, not without its general. Soon enough the British will put an end to it. And to us. Without an army of our own, we may as well be prostrate before them. The lion will show no mercy, of that I am quite certain." Then Dr. Franklin puts a finger under his collar, as if he can already feel the noose tightening.

It is Elizabeth who breaks the impasse. "It is his device, sir—his contrivance—that has brought him here. And that, with your help, can be made to undo what has been done."

"Can it?" Dr. Franklin asks me. "Can it do as she claims?"

"It can do something," I say. "Otherwise, how could I be here in the first place?"

Mr. Farrington is puzzled and begs for answers, but no one takes the time to bring him up to speed, as we are certain that he can be of no help whatsoever.

"You ask me?" says Dr. Franklin. "I scarcely believe your tale at all. But now a part of it—the essential part of it—is confirmed. General Washington is dead. But the rest of it? What proof have you?"

"I am the proof. I know things that could not possibly be known. You—all of you—are my history, my past. And I have the device with me. The iPhone. I was holding it in my hand . . . when . . . when . . . something happened."

"And what, precisely, happened, pray tell?"

I think about it. It's hard to remember. Foggy, in my mind, in my memory. But: "There were three of us. Me, Bev, and Brandon."

"We've seen them," said Daniel. "At the farm. They were captured by the Germans."

"Right," I say. "But before then . . . we had come in a minivan to watch the reenactment. Which was kind of pathetic, if you want to know the truth. Because we were left behind—on Christmas Day, no less. Our parents were kind of too busy. So the school was taking care of us."

"School?" says Sally. "What school?"

"Minivan?" says Mr. Farrington. "What is a minivan?"

"Reenactment?" says Dr. Franklin. "What is this?"

"A minivan is a kind of car," I say. "It has an engine inside, an internal combustion engine that runs on gasoline and propels the car along. The school is the Fredericksville School, which is where we go. And a reenactment is when a bunch of people get dressed up and pretend they're people from a different time period. For example, if you got dressed up like Pilgrims, you might *reenact* the

Mayflower landing. So every Christmas, thousands of people gather. To watch a bunch of . . . reenactors . . . cross the Delaware. In longboats. Just like Washington did, on Christmas night of this year. Then they marched into Trenton, where they routed the Hessians and changed the course of the war."

"My Lord," says Dr. Franklin. He picks up his pen and dips the tip into the inkwell. "An internal combustion engine? How exactly does it work?"

"Father," says Sally, "let us keep our eyes on the main chance, shall we?"

"We could make ourselves a tidy fortune," he says to her, "a tidy fortune indeed, if we knew a quarter of what this young man says."

"Father, Father," Sally says, shaking her head. "A fortune, tidy or otherwise, is quite beside the point, don't you think?"

"A fortune is never beside the point, my dear," Dr. Franklin says. "Ahem: 'An investment in knowledge always pays the best interest.' *Poor Richard's Almanac,* I should guess 1752." He waves his hand. "But in any case. Carry on, young man. Pay no mind to me."

"So I'm trying to piece this together. . . . We're walking around, watching the reenactors getting ready. It's a beautiful, sunny day, kind of warm for Christmas, but then it hasn't snowed on Christmas in years—I don't suppose anyone's heard of global warming, but let's not go there—and then we stop at the general store, where they were serving free apple cider. This general store is a touristy place, they sell books and knickknacks and fake muskets for kids and tricornered hats. And laminated copies of both the Declaration of Independence and the Constitution."

"The constitution?" says Dr. Franklin. "Of what?"

"Of these United States," I say. "It comes later, in 1787. The Constitution is what establishes us as a nation. I had to memorize the preamble to the Constitution when I was in the fifth grade. Want to hear it?"

There being no objection, I begin: "We the people," I say, "of the United States, in order to form a more perfect union, establish justice, insure domestic tranquility, provide for the common defense, promote the general welfare, and secure the blessings of liberty to ourselves and our posterity, do ordain and establish this constitution of the United States of America."

"Hear, hear!" Dr. Franklin says, and gives two raps upon the floor with his cane. "Hear, hear. I support those sentiments in their entirety. Well said!"

THIRTY

B UT I HAVE TO finish my story. "Anyway," I say. "So we're in this general store. And now I remember something—we were really bored. It was Christmas, remember, and maybe all of us were feeling a little terrible, you know, that we had to spend Christmas, of all days, with each other instead of our families. Anyway, we see this old guy scurrying out from the basement of the general store, and Brandon *dares* us to find out what the old man is up to.

"We walk down this rickety wooden staircase to the basement, which is, like, two hundred and fifty years old. Cobwebs all over. We're all getting the creeps, but it's also kind of fun. So there's like two rooms. The first room is kind of what we'd expect—dirt floor, old stuff all over, smelly, cobwebs, and dark. We have to use our phones to light the place up. But then Brandon notices another room. Smaller, with a door. And definitely a light on inside. He tries to open the door, but it's locked. So he grabs the doorknob and basically breaks in. Then he says, 'Whoops.'

"We go inside. There's a small table, and a chair. And on the table is a"—I'm about to say a MacBook, but of course no one will know what that is. I think for a moment. "Well, there's basically a much bigger version of this," I say, holding up my iPhone. "Much bigger, and much more powerful. So anyway, Brandon starts poking around. Now, we're all figuring that this is the old guy's, uh, machine, the old guy Brandon saw, but it's weird, because what's up with that? Does the old guy *live* in the basement of the general store or something? And now I remember what happened next very clearly: Brandon must have hit the wrong button. I don't know what he did, but I remember what he said. He said: 'Uh-oh.' Like he'd just done something wrong.

"All of our iPhones start going haywire. Lighting up, going on and off, and then they start beeping—but not beeps we've heard before, because you can select your own beeps, you know?"

They don't know; I remember that none of them have ever heard, let alone selected, an electronic beep of any kind, so I continue. "All right. Then our phones, like, start talking to each other. Communicate somehow, or send a signal. 'Cause all three phones start doing the hay-wire thing, but in some sort of sequence, or pattern—like they're all being *programmed* or something. And all of this is happening right after Brandon pushed some buttons on the guy's machine and said uh-oh. Then the room starts twirling around. It's weird, 'cause I had completely forgotten about this till now. Next thing is, we're in this stable someplace. And it's, like, really, really cold, you know? It takes us a couple of minutes to get oriented, then we start poking around, checking out what's what. That's when we see him. General Washington. Lying dead, in a horse stall, though it was pretty obvious that whoever had shot him had just done it. The blood was . . . you know . . . still fresh."

Dr. Franklin holds his hand out once more. "Let me examine your device . . . once again, if I may."

I turn it on and hand it to him. "There's more stuff," I say. "Just swipe it, like this, with your finger."

He swipes my phone, and sees what I have on page two.

And page three.

And page four.

"What, may I ask," he says, "are these symbols?"

"Those," I answer, "are called apps. Short for applications. Programs that make it do stuff."

"So how does one . . . cause one of these *apps,* as you call them . . . to initiate?"

"Just touch one of them," I say.

"With what?"

"With your finger. Just tap it once, not too hard, not too soft."

And so the great Dr. Benjamin Franklin, inventor, signer of the Declaration and the Constitution, taps an app on my iPhone. He taps it once, not too hard, not too soft.

And opens Angry Birds.

"What in heaven's name," says Dr. Franklin, "is all this squawking racket?"

THIRTY-ONE

"**T**AP HERE," I SAY, pointing to the home button. "It'll get rid of that. It's just a game, by the way. To pass the time."

Dr. Franklin peers at me over his half-rimmed spectacles and frowns. He doesn't even have to tell me what he's thinking. I know. I know full well. *All this incredible technology . . . and you waste your time with that silly game?* It's pretty much the exact same thing my dad—and every one of my teachers—says all the time.

"Very well," he says. "Perhaps you should describe for me . . . the utility . . . of these *apps* of yours. Before I do any further—what do you say?—*tapping*. What, pray tell, is this one? *iTunes?*"

"That's for music," I say. "To listen to anytime you want."

"Most ingenious," Dr. Franklin says, and taps the iTunes icon. Up it pops, and the first song he sees, he doesn't like. "'American Idiot'? Good Lord, what is that?"

"Just an old song," I say. "I don't even listen to it anymore."

"'American Idiot'? By Green Day? What is Green Day?"

"Just a punk band, sir, but they're not that cool anymore. I should probably delete that one."

"And this one? Lady . . . Lady *Gaga*?"

"That's a mistake," I say quickly. "I don't even know how that got there."

He frowns again—and he rolls his eyes. "I shall tap no more," he says. "This device is most disturbing indeed. But I see there are useful functions: *Mail, Notes, Clock, Calendar*, and so forth. Pray tell, what is this one? iTime?"

"iTime? I don't think . . . I didn't know . . . that I have an app called iTime." I check my phone, and sure enough, there it is. A pale blue background, and a white arrow, pointing in both directions, across the middle. "I never downloaded that," I say. "I've never seen it before, either."

I notice we're down to one percent power, the lowest I've ever been. "Dr. Franklin," I say, "we have to turn this off. Once it loses power it will be useless. We have to figure out a way to recharge it. Then we can see what iTime is all about." I take the phone from his hands, turn it off. Then I show him the battery slot on the bottom of the phone. "See this? That's where the charger goes. One end fits right in, and the other end basically goes into a wall outlet. And a wall outlet, before you ask, is how every home gets electricity. Every house has four or five wall outlets in every room. You plug your wire into the wall outlet, and voilà—all the electricity you could ever want."

He wants his paper and pen again. "I must write this all down," he says. "Fascinating. Tell me: is there a fee, for the use of these wall outlets?"

"Dr. Franklin," I say, "if you can get my phone fully recharged, I promise to tell you everything I know, and you're free to do whatever you want with it."

He closes his eyes, and then the great man nods. "I think," he says, "it may be possible, but I make no guarantee."

That's going to have to be good enough. For now, anyway.

THIRTY-TWO

ONE HOUR LATER, WE'RE in a print shop on Market Street that was once owned by Dr. Franklin but at present is managed by Mr. Farrington. We had to haul Dr. Franklin under a cover in our one-horse shay, which did not seem to please our one horse, good old Juniper. There wasn't enough room on the bench for either Elizabeth or me, so while Daniel hauled Dr. Franklin down Market Street, we walked through the snow.

We're all crowded around now in a back room of the print shop—Dr. Franklin, Mr. Farrington, Daniel, Elizabeth, and me. All we have to do is come up with a way to recharge my phone, fiddle around a little, then fix a monumental historical error—and the sooner, the better.

No biggie, right?

My iPhone is on the table, and Dr. Franklin and Mr. Farrington each have a big magnifying glass, and they are peering at things. And asking questions. Questions a reasonable person might reasonably expect the owner of the thing to know a little bit about.

Such as: "What's it made of? Is the material found in nature, or is it manufactured?"

"If manufactured, how so? In a foundry? Through what process? How is the material shaped?"

"How is it bent?"

"How long does it take to cool off?"

"Would it melt if left out in the sun?"

"Would it freeze if left out in the cold?"

"How long does it take to make one?"

"How many are made at a time?"

"It appears that the face of the device is glass. How is the glass fitted to the other material, which, since you don't know, is of indeterminate origin?"

"What happens if the glass breaks?"

Elizabeth decides to join in the fun. "On the back of it," she says, "there is an engraving of an apple, with a bite taken out of its right side. Why so? Did someone eat it? If so, why?"

I give Elizabeth a quick glare, to no effect.

Then Daniel chimes in. "There are holes," he says, "in the bottom. Why?"

I tell them one is for the earbuds, and the other is for the charger. Don't worry about the earbud plug, I say. I'll explain that some other time. It's the charger slot we have to focus on.

They spend a good deal of time peering at the charger slot. Naturally they have more questions. They want me to describe, in precise detail, each item used in the recharging process, even if I don't know their official names. I say you put one end of the charger into the end of the phone and the other end you plug into a wall outlet.

What could be simpler?

Finally Dr. Franklin puts down his magnifying glass. "Tell me, lad," he says. "How does one . . . open . . . this device? There does not seem to be any . . . pathway, as it were . . . to the interior."

"I have it," says Mr. Farrington, peering through his magnifying glass. "On the bottom here. Two tiny screws. Perhaps . . . if we were . . . to unscrew them . . . the back itself could be lifted off? And then gain full access to its innards, perhaps."

A low murmur, as Dr. Franklin and Mr. Farrington consult. "Capital idea," Dr. Franklin says. "Capital!"

"The seed, sir, from you. But let me make haste. I shall return most expeditiously." Then Mr. Farrington puts on his winter cloak, his hat, and a scarf, and is off.

"Where's he going?" I ask.

"He's off to get assistance," Dr. Franklin explains. "From his brother-in-law, a Mr. William Topping. Who, as luck would have it, is a clockmaker. He shall bring his tools, and we shall pry our way into this . . . this . . . *iPhone.* And we shall see what we shall see."

"Okay," I say, though I'm pretty sure gaining full access to the innards is going to void my warranty. But then we all have to make sacrifices in times like these, right?

THIRTY-THREE

Forty-five minutes later Mr. Farrington returns with his brother-in-law, Mr. William Topping, clockmaker. Mr. Topping is nearly as old as Dr. Franklin. His face is red, from coming over in the cold and snow, and he is decidedly cheerful.

"Very delighted to meet you, young man, very delighted indeed! A rare pleasure, a rare pleasure to be sure! And you are from where?"

"New Jersey," I say, offering my hand, which he gives a hearty pump. "Basically."

"Basically from New Jersey? My word! Did you hear that, Franklin? The young man is *basically* from New Jersey! Har-har-har!"

Dr. Franklin forces a tepid quarter smile. "Topping,"

he says, "we have before us a device whose exact provenance is unknown, and at this moment unimportant. What must be done to open it, Topping? That is our only relevant concern."

"Opening it," Mr. Topping says, "is but half the problem, Franklin. Do you seek to have it closed as well?"

"Closed?"

"Closed. After you've opened it, you do want it closed back up, yes?"

"Naturally," Dr. Franklin says. "This is why we brought you, Topping. With the hope that you would not simply lop the thing in two with a meat cleaver. A delicate hand, Mr. Topping. Nothing is to be altered or tampered with. And yes, of course: what you undo must be made whole again, in as perfect a form as you see before you."

"Very well," Mr. Topping says. "Then I shall need, firstly, a high chair to sit upon, and a small glass of rum, if you please, to steady my fingers. Secondly, we shall need to discuss my fee. Upon successful completion of the task you've given me, Franklin, I shall expect no less than two guineas."

"I shall give you one, Topping," Dr. Franklin says. "And you shall be happy with it. If not, away with you, and I will find someone else to do it for half the price."

Mr. Topping shrugs. A high chair is brought to him, and so is a small glass of rum. He takes some tools out of his leather bag, and thirty seconds later the front cover is off and the iPhone lays exposed.

"Ah," says Dr. Franklin. "The thing's entrails. Most interesting." He picks up his magnifying glass, and the next thing I know Mr. Farrington is taking wires out of a box. And I didn't even know they had wires in 1776.

"Tell me," Dr. Franklin says, "what call you the differences? Between charges, that is. When I began my investigations into the nature of electricity, I had the most vexing time referring to things, or indeed discussing my findings with anyone else. Nothing was named, you see. No common terms. Of course I did what I could—I called the one end the positive charge, the other end the negative—poor terms, perhaps, but they were the best I could devise. What call you these things? In . . . your day?"

"We call them the same," I say. "Positive and negative."

"Well," Dr. Franklin says, and smiles. "I can't say I am displeased, though I should have thought to patent the terms." So then he asks: "How is the current from the wall outlet regulated?

"Are the positive and negative charges channeled to corresponding poles in the device that plugs into the bottom of the iPhone?

"Are there positive and negative receptors inside the iPhone which accept the corresponding positive and negative charges from the charging device?"

I've never thought about any of these questions—I just plug the thing in—but I try to answer as best I can. Then Dr. Franklin says, under his breath, "This wire here,

Topping, will be the negative conductor. I ask you not to question my judgment, but merely to affix the end of the wire to that . . . to that . . . curved portion . . . there. Can you do it, Topping? Without argument? And when you are quite done, repeat the process, with the other wire, to the similar curved portion on the other side. When you are finished, we shall be able to convey electricity into the device."

"But how shall you provide it electricity, Dr. Franklin?" asks Daniel. "There is no storm and no lightning. Must we wait?"

"We are able to generate our own, young man," Dr. Franklin says. "Unfortunately, we cannot bring our electricity to the device. We must bring the device to our electricity. Mr. Farrington, if you please. Let us do so at this very moment."

My iPhone lies on its back, its front side exposed, with two long, thin wires protruding from it. Mr. Farrington picks it up, and we go to the front of the print shop, where there is a very large wooden box, as big as a mahogany chest. But at the very top of the chest is a shelf, and upon the shelf are about three dozen big glass jars. Five rows of seven, to be exact. And each jar has a funny-looking lid with metal rods crisscrossing the entire contraption.

Dr. Franklin is beaming, as if he himself is lit up. "Behold!" he says. "Our storehouse of electricity! Mr. Farrington, if you please: engage the condensers!"

THIRTY-FOUR

F OR A GUY WHO was there at the creation of American democracy, he sure as heck didn't give me a vote. Because the next thing I know, my iPhone is being hooked up. By the two wires dangling out of its back to the big chest of glass jars.

"Don't be so alarmed, young man," Dr. Franklin says. "'Tis perfectly safe. The jars you see are called Leyden jars, and they were originally devised in Holland. It was my conceit to bunch them together. Do you know one year, using this device, we electrified a turkey? It was most uncommon tasty, if a cook be allowed to praise his own cookery. So moist, so tender: a memorable meal. So my electrical battery is able to generate electricity, of that there is no doubt. And we know electricity is able to flow through wires, such wires as we have affixed to your device. But we must be able to determine if our experiment be successful, do we not? But we do not have a turkey at hand, whose results we are able to see as well as to eat. Have you any suggestions, young man? How we may know if we are, at this moment . . . injecting . . . your device with all the electricity it needs?"

"It'll turn on by itself, and start recharging," I say. "We won't have to do a thing."

Which is exactly what all of us do.

I can hardly believe my eyes.

It's charging. The power bar moves!

I'd like to see the *MythBusters* people try this one.

It's at five percent power, and gaining by the second.

"I knew Dr. Franklin could do it," Elizabeth says. "I had no doubt of it."

"How long shall it take?" Daniel asks.

"An hour," I say. "Two hours? Something like that."

"A more precise calculation would be helpful," Dr. Franklin says. "Our Leyden jars will not last forever."

"It has to get to at least fifty percent," I say. "Mr. Hart said so."

"Mr. Hart?"

"He's my teacher. Somehow . . . we're able to text each other. But not call."

"Text?"

"Yeah. Send short messages."

"Using this device?"

"Yes."

"If you tell me," Dr. Franklin says, "that you are capable of communicating . . . with someone . . . not of here . . . but of . . . your time . . . if you tell me this, young man, I believe I shall expire on the spot."

"All right," I say. "I won't tell you then."

He waits. But I know well enough by now that he won't wait for long. He's too curious to wait for anything.

"All right, confound it," he says. "Go ahead and communicate with this Mr. Hart of yours. Tell him Dr. Benjamin Franklin sends his compliments."

I pick up my phone and text Mr. Hart. *Dr. Franklin is helping. Now at 20 percent power.*

We wait, but there is no answer. And while we're waiting, I get an awful feeling: maybe there'll *never* be an answer. If George Washington is dead, wouldn't the whole history of the world be permanently altered? And if so, how long would it take to . . . to . . . *manifest* itself?

The minutes go by. Every once in a while I pick up the phone, to see if a text has arrived, though I know full well that a familiar electronic beep would let me know. And I check the power status: thirty percent. Forty. Forty-five. Fifty. Fifty-five.

And that might be all we are going to get. Because we are now beginning to notice something. People, in the street, just outside the shop.

Not ordinary people, either.

Agitated people.

THIRTY-FIVE

And we all know why: the news of General Washington's demise is being carried along, person to person, family to family, neighbor to neighbor, by the fastest way possible: word of mouth. Everyone wants to be the first to tell the news; no one wants to be the last to hear.

And I'm now at just about sixty percent power. "Do you think you have a sufficient supply?" Dr. Franklin asks.

"I think," I say, "that what I have is going to have to be good enough."

"I am beginning to sense," Dr. Franklin says, and his eyes scan the street, which is filling rapidly with passersby, "that our experiment has come to its conclusion. I fear my cabinet of Leyden jars—my electrical battery—has never been put to such a test. I also suspect we will not be permitted the leisure of standing here for so long a time without distraction. Indeed, I keenly feel a fresh distraction approaches us at this very moment."

He isn't wrong. Into the shop come a group of men, four of them, and they make no effort to hide the alarm on their faces.

Daniel nudges me. "Patriots," he says. "By which I mean fellow revolutionaries of Dr. Franklin's."

"Dr. Franklin!" cries the first. "Have you heard the awful news? General Washington is killed!"

"I have already heard this unbearably awful news, Samuel," Dr. Franklin says. "Time and time again. I suspect every man, woman, and child in Philadelphia has heard by now."

"The people are saying the revolution is finished, that we must sue the king for peace. What are we to do now, Dr. Franklin?" Samuel says. He is a younger man, perhaps the same age as Mr. Farrington—thirty, I would guess.

"This is the question of the hour, Samuel. His death is confirmed?"

"It is, alas. His body has been recovered and protected."

"Protected?"

"His staff is fearful, Dr. Franklin. That . . . unruly bands . . . will seek to desecrate . . . the lifeless body of a man they used to fear and respect. I speak not of the populace, sir. Who present their own problems. I speak of General Washington's unpaid soldiers, who are using this event as license to unleash their more degenerate passions. The stores of rum and grog, sir, have been breached. None would have dared were Washington alive."

"The army . . . ," Dr. Franklin says, hesitating. "Can it not be restored to order?"

"I believe it too late, sir. Their complaint is that since they are unpaid, and due, they are no longer subject. They have sprung themselves upon the populace, like winter locusts, and are intent on taking, from whosoever shall have plenty, that which they deem their due. What keeps these soldiers yoked, sir, is the order and discipline of the army. The yoke has been removed; they are roaming, and pillaging, at will. I fear our revolution, Dr. Franklin, is unraveling at a frightful pace. If only providence would undo what has been done!"

"Rest assured, Samuel," Dr. Franklin says. "We are engaged in the very thing. Young man," he says, turning to me, "the toll is rising, and may rise far more than we ever could fear. Are you not sufficiently supplied . . . for us to carry on?"

I check my iPhone and see I'm at seventy percent. "We're good," I say. Which is exactly what I know Dr. Franklin wants to hear.

What he certainly doesn't want to hear is what we hear next: a crowd approaching us from down the street. Samuel, Daniel, and Mr. Farrington open the door, and their faces are aghast; we are, Samuel says, in proximate danger. And Mr. Topping, it appears, has somehow managed to slip away, when no one was paying attention.

We hear the crowd. They are chanting the same thing, over and over: "Death to traitors! Death to traitors! Long live the king!"

THIRTY-SIX

"**D**ISENTANGLE THE WIRES!" DR. Franklin says to Mr. Farrington. "Put it back together! We shall grab the device and go! Through the back! Mr. Farrington, if you please: fortify the front. Let us not be detected or disturbed. The future of our revolution depends upon it!"

I hold the iPhone while Mr. Farrington detaches the wires and puts the cover on, and then we leave the whole Leyden jar battery cabinet contraption behind and hustle off to the back room.

"Hustle," of course, is a relative term. Daniel, Elizabeth, and I are perfectly capable; Dr. Franklin, not so much. He does a kind of half-shuffle hopalong, using his cane as a pivot point and a launch tool, but we get there. With maybe two seconds to spare.

As we duck into the back room, Samuel and his comrades, directed by Mr. Farrington, stand foursquare inside the front door, blocking any penetration. We hear the chant—"Death to traitors, death to traitors, long live the King"—and we hear the door being rattled.

"Hurry!" says Daniel. "Hurry, Mel! We haven't much time!"

We exit the print shop through a little-used back door and trudge through snowdrifts, with Dr. Franklin shouting directions. Daniel leads the way; Elizabeth and I are alongside Dr. Franklin, helping him, or at least trying to help him, keep pace.

We have to tromp through snow, back-alley snow, and it's cold. We can hear the crowd, fading away now, but still chanting: "Death to traitors! Long live the king!" We all hope that Mr. Farrington and Samuel's men have been able to fend them off, because if they come after us, in these narrow alleyways, going at Dr. Franklin's pace— we'll all be dead meat.

Dr. Franklin shouts to Daniel to turn right, then right again; we come to the end of an alley, and to a back door. Daniel knocks on the door, and he knocks again, and then the door is opened a crack and we are let in.

The house belongs to an older woman, maybe as old as Dr. Franklin himself. She isn't introduced—there isn't time—nor does she stick around. We're let in, the door is closed, and Dr. Franklin glances out the window.

"Our tracks," he says, "cannot be hidden, or obscured.

Should the mob burst through, it won't take them long to find us, and I fear our time will have come to an end. Mel, we have electrified your device as well as we could; the moment has arrived for you to command it to do what it can do, or for us to discover . . . the futility of our efforts. Mel? Please proceed."

All eyes are upon me. I take my iPhone in my hand, and with one only slightly trembling right forefinger I press the mysterious icon that says iTime.

THIRTY-SEVEN

M<small>Y</small> I<small>PHONE</small> <small>KIND OF BUZZES</small>. Kind of shakes, rattles, and rolls.

Then a simple screen appears. And on the screen, a message. It says this:

Welcome to iTIME.

Brought to You by T.G.W., Inc.

The Aim Is to Play.

To Mess About.

Who Says Things Have to Be This Way and Not Another?

Who Says Things Wouldn't Be Better if a Different Road Had Been Taken?

Catch Us if You Can.

K.

We read this, and as we do the message fizzles away and disappears. A new screen appears. Five large boxes.

And, to the far right, at the lower corner, a little green circle. And in the middle of the little green circle, tiny letters, etched in white: *Submit*.

"I fear I don't understand," says Dr. Franklin, "the point of the message. I wish to reread it. Mel—can we?"

I try to, but I can't get the message back. I hit the home button, then iTime again, but no message. Just the five large boxes, and the one small circle.

"It said something about T.G.W., Inc." says Daniel. "What is that?"

"I don't know," I say.

"It was also signed, I think," says Elizabeth. "By someone named 'K.' Who is this?"

"Presumably," says Dr. Franklin, "the inventor. And I know something about inventing. You always wish to leave your mark, somehow. Credit must be given where credit is due. So let us assume that 'K' is the inventor, and the message, cryptic though it be, is for us. Now then. Let us continue our examination."

All of us are peering intently at the little electronic screen on the odd little device sitting in the palm of my left hand. A thing I do fifty, seventy-five times a day. A thing none of them, essentially, have ever done.

Box one, on the left: DAY. Inside the box is *25*.

Box two: MONTH. Inside the box, *12*.

Box three: YEAR. Inside the box, *1776*.

Box four: TIME. Inside the box, *11:00*.

Box five: COORDINATES. Inside the box, *+40.287660, -74.8898391*.

That's it. No other information to go by, no instructions, no tabs.

Dr. Franklin speaks first. "Mel," he says. "At what time did you . . . arrive on Christmas Day?"

"I don't remember exactly," I say. "But eleven o'clock in the morning seems about right."

Dr. Franklin nods. Then he puts a hand on my shoulder. "Tell me, Mel," he says. "What do you think would happen if you changed the setting? On this device? If we were to put in ten o'clock, let us say, in the box on the right? In place of eleven o'clock?"

"I would guess I might have an hour to work with."

"Indeed," Dr. Franklin says. "And if that were so, Mel, do you think that you would be able to . . . handle things?"

Dr. Franklin's eyes are on mine. He sees a twelve-year-old kid, a skinny kid, a kid with braces on his teeth. He's really asking, does it make sense to trust this entire operation to a twelve-year-old *boy*?

I remember what my dad said: You want to be *somebody*, right? You don't just want to be a *potted plant*, do you? What he didn't tell me was that there'd be an occasion when you don't have much of a choice, like right now. When you'd be forced to do something you never knew you had in you.

"Don't worry, Dr. Franklin," I say, and hold his gaze steadily. "I got it covered."

THIRTY-EIGHT

ELIZABETH COMES FORWARD AND puts her hand on my arm. "He'll know what to do, Dr. Franklin," she says. "He's gotten us this far." Then she does something very strange, and very nice: she hugs me. For all she's worth.

She's also tearing up a little, and it hits me. This is going to be the end of something, isn't it?

Dr. Franklin understands it. So does Daniel.

If I reset the time, to one hour earlier—for us, everything changes.

"Tell me," Dr. Franklin says. "Indulge an old man. Are we remembered?"

"To this day," I say. "Celebrated and honored. Your picture, Dr. Franklin, is on our one hundred dollar bill. One of the most popular science museums in Philadelphia is called the Franklin Institute. Every kid in America learns about you, sir, to this day. And they will for every day to come."

"My picture," he says, "on a hundred dollar bill. I can't imagine. I am speechless, I truly am." And then Dr. Franklin positively beams.

But then we hear them—the mob. They've found our tracks in the snow. It won't be long till they find us.

I push the TIME box, and reset it to "10:00."

There's only one thing left to do: press the little green circle in the lower right corner. *Submit*.

And I can't bring myself to do it just yet.

There is more to say.

To explain.

"Wait," says Daniel. "I want to come with you. Elizabeth can stay behind."

"I will not!" Elizabeth says. "We shall go together."

"I don't think so," I say. "It's a one-person operation." I'm not absolutely certain about this, but at this point I don't want to take any chances. Besides, it would completely blow everyone's brains to bits if *this* Daniel and Elizabeth happened to run into *that* Daniel and Elizabeth.

Which I realize makes absolutely no sense at all, except for the fact that it does.

"I've learned wonders, absolute wonders," Dr. Franklin says. "A veritable fortune could be had, a hundred fortunes could be had, if I have retained a tenth of it. But I fear not. Mel—are you thinking along the same lines as I? Once you . . . go back . . . all this . . . will be as if it never were?"

"Dr. Franklin, I think you're right—all of this, and all you've learned, will be as if it never happened."

We can not only hear the mob now, but also see them. They've got muskets, sticks, and torches. What they plan to do with all of it I don't want to know. They are chanting, "Death to traitors, death to traitors, long live the king."

I put my finger on the green circle.

I give a final nod to Elizabeth, to Daniel, and to Dr. Franklin.

"You must go," Dr. Franklin says. "You must go this instant, before it is too late! They approach! Good luck to you, lad! For the revolution!"

"For the revolution!" I say, and press the green circle.

My phone starts tingling, buzzing. It goes completely haywire, and the room starts twirling around and around and around.

Then I'm gone.

THE TIME BEFORE
THAT TIME

THIRTY-NINE

I T'S KIND OF LIKE I clicked my heels together three times, and said: "I am not a potted plant.

"I am not a potted plant.

"I am not a potted plant, Dad."

Then I'm in a stable. A very familiar stable.

There are stacks of hay, saddles hanging up on a wall, bunches of rope, and a godawful stench.

And though I'm dizzy and disoriented and still feel like everything is spinning round and round and round, there's something I just have to know.

Is that stall empty?

Or no?

I know where it is. I don't have to search around. In less than a second I find it.

No dead bodies anywhere.

So that leaves a two-item agenda. Item number one: make sure no one shoots and kills General George Washington.

Item two: make sure that at exactly eleven o'clock—one hour from now—I'm in this stable, at this same spot.

'Cause I expect two—or maybe three—befuddled prep school kids to crash-land after a whirling ride of 240-odd years. What I'll do is tell 'em what's what, who's who, get everyone to reprogram our iPhones, and get the heck out of here and back to where we belong. General Washington will have to carry on by himself.

I say maybe three, because what if, at eleven o'clock, I see not only Brandon and Bev, but also me?

Is that even possible?

It would be weird. Because that me would not be the me I'd want to be. Get it?

This is the me that knows stuff. That got the iPhone powered up, and figured out the iTime app. Any other me walking around would just get in the way.

So I have an hour to figure everything out. Or even less than that, because I just wasted a good five minutes standing around the stall and looking at nothing but hay.

FORTY

OUTSIDE THE STABLE, IT'S all snow, all white, just like it was last time. Of course I know the layout and terrain. But now my clothes are different. I'm wearing the coat and pants Daniel gave me, and my white Nikes. Which definitely are going to stand out, but that's probably the very least important thing on my agenda.

I can't just wait here. I have to think this through. Somehow, their plan is to get Washington into the stable, where they can shoot him. So that means right now they have to be either on their way or very close by.

I exit the stable on the right, same as last time. I go about thirty yards through the snow. No Brandon to plow the way, so it's tough going. I head off to the right, and tromp through another twenty yards or so of snow, until it flattens out somewhat and I come to what I know is a snow-covered path. The snow here isn't quite so deep, isn't quite so tiring to trudge through.

The pathway angles up. Then angles down, to the farmhouse below.

The house is made of stone. Not too big, not too fancy. Smoke is pouring out of a chimney.

And, patrolling in front, two Hessians. The same two guys as the last time I was here. The same two dumb gold cone hats on their heads.

Unfortunately, they've already spotted me.

But they don't raise their muskets and fire. Oh no. They do something most unexpected, and strange: they smile and wave.

And it hits me: what do they have to be afraid of? I'm just a *kid*, like any other kid. Maybe they think I'm part of the family.

"Hallo!" one of them hollers. English, but a heavy German accent. "Hallo!"

I can't think of anything to do except wave back.

Then he makes a gesture, like he's eating something. "Food!" he shouts. "Food, food!" Then he waves his hand, like he's inviting me in.

I kind of figure at this point the dude's English consists of maybe two words.

I'm pretty sure I don't want to have anything to do with German food, but I can't think of any way to get out of it. I trudge down the hill; to the farmhouse I go. The two Hessians are still smiling, still waving. But as I get closer to them I'm able to see their eyes, which are not smiling, not waving.

Oh.

These are the eyes of soldiers on duty. Wary. Suspicious. And one other thing I'm pretty sure of: *in the know.*

They'd have to be.

They've been posted at the farmhouse to keep watch on things while the other ones—the faux colonial farmers—are off executing the mission.

So a kid, like me, walking around the farm?

A *problem.*

A potential *hazard.*

An *eyewitness.*

Here, kid. Come and get it. A nice little *biscuit.*

I'm maybe fifteen yards away from them now.

The one who shouted "Food, food!" has his hands out, a fake smile plastered on his face. They still have the same rotten stubby teeth, and I can smell them from here.

The other one, who hasn't said a word, has his hands on his musket. At the end of which is a bayonet. Which I know he's itching to stick right through me, and he can't wait for me to get close enough so he can.

Payback.

Because if I'm not mistaken, this is the exact same dude I myself stomach butted the last time I was here.

Which was an hour in the future.

So he wants payback for something that hasn't happened yet?

Doesn't seem sporting of the guy, if you ask me.

But I can see his fingers. And they're twitching. Like he just can't wait.

I'm eight, nine yards away now.

I'm past the point of turning tail and running, because they have muskets, which fire musket balls, which can go faster than I can run.

I can only think of one thing to do.

"Daniel!" I call. "Elizabeth! I could use some help here!"

FORTY-ONE

NOTHING.

Dead silence.

I try again. "Daniel? Elizabeth? You there?"

I'm six yards away from these guys, and I'm not taking another step forward. And I'm thinking: I can't let them know that *I* know they're in the middle of a mission. So I have to do everything I can to convince them that I'm just a kid. Inconsequential. That is, no one to be afraid of, or concerned about.

Just a kid, walking around.

"Food, food," says the one. He waves me closer.

"Daniel?" I say. "Elizabeth? If you guys can hear me, I could really use some help. Like, right about now."

Twitchy Fingers takes a step toward me. One more

step and he'll be able to reach out and grab me by my coat.

Then I hear them.

Daniel and Elizabeth. They must have been, like I figured, watching the whole time.

"Hello, hello!" Daniel hollers, from up the hill. "We're over here! Come and play!"

That's plenty good enough for me. I nod to Hessian One and Hessian Two, wave my hand, turn around, and take off.

But merrily, if you can believe it.

I'm just a kid, and I'm just here to play. Not even Hessians would shoot down a kid romping around in the snow, would they?

Ahead, at the crest of the hill, are Daniel and Elizabeth, arms tightly folded across their chests, frowns upon their faces.

"Who in the world," she says, "are you? And what are you doing on our property? And how do you know who we are? And why did you call our names as if wanting us to rescue you from . . . from them?"

Daniel says nothing at first, though he does look down at my feet and sees my white Nikes.

I'm not so sure I can keep a smile off my face. I'm very happy to see them, after all. We had ourselves a wonderful adventure in Dr. Franklin's Philadelphia. Too bad they don't know a thing about it.

"I feel like we're old friends," I say.

"How dare you!" Elizabeth says. "We've never seen the

likes of you in our lives! The—the—audacity! Using our names—as if we know you—without our permission—on our property. . . . There are laws! These kinds of actions are not permissible! They are not acceptable! State your name at once, or we shall—or we shall . . . I don't know what we shall do, but we shall do something!"

"My name," I say, and hold out my hand, "is Mel. And I am very, very pleased to meet you. Honored, I would even say. I feel like I've known you both a very long time."

Elizabeth wants nothing to do with shaking my hand, but Daniel relents and does. "Good morning to you, Mel," he says. "May I ask what brings you to—to—"

"Whatever are those—those *things* on your feet?" interrupts Elizabeth.

"They're called *sneakers*," I say. "Everyone wears them these days."

"I've never seen such things before in my life."

"Well, maybe they're not that common around here. But give it time."

"You are on *our* farm," Elizabeth says. "Without our permission. And I am *quite* certain we have never met." She takes a step closer, inspecting me like a piece of suspect meat. "What is your family name? And your business on our farm?"

"I'm Mel," I say. "Just Mel. I basically come from New Jersey. And my business on this farm is simple: we are going to have to save General George Washington. If we do not, he will be dead within the hour, and the revolution will die with him."

FORTY-TWO

MOUTHS, AS THEY SAY, fly open. First Daniel's, then Elizabeth's.

"You say what?" Elizabeth says. "You say what about General Washington?"

"Look," I say. "One thing we don't have is a lot of time. Your father rented this farm to what he thought were innocent German farmers, but they're not. They are on a secret mission—to kill General Washington and thereby end this revolution. They're led by a guy that's short, ugly, and has a crooked nose. And he carries a very strange pistol. Their plan is to get General Washington back to this farm somehow and then they are going to lure him into the horse stable, shoot him, and leave him there stone-cold dead. This is happening *as we speak*. And we three are the only ones in this world who will be able to do something about it. Now—do I need to explain anything else? Or are you two ready to help?"

Though Elizabeth maintains her glare and her anger, Daniel does not. The expression on his face changes at once, and he very nearly slaps his forehead. "Of course!" he says. "It makes perfect sense! The horses!"

"The horses?" Elizabeth and I say, in perfect unison.

"Yes! The horses! The one—the short ugly one with the crooked nose—the one who gave Father gold—was asking me about our horses. I told him they were all gone—sold to the Continental Army—and that the price should have been dear but was not, for want of currency. He asked me if the horses had been stolen, and I said they had not been, nor had they been paid for properly either. A note, is what the officer told Father. A promissory note, backed by the full faith and credit of the Continental Congress, which has neither faith nor credit. But the horses were taken—seven of them. They promised to return them intact if they could. But what the German gentleman was asking was what if we possessed a dozen or more magnificent horses—would we be able to sell them to the army? And I said if that were so, General Washington himself would make the transaction personally—everyone knows the general's love for horses. They could have enticed him here easily. To see horses that do not exist."

"And this German guy," I ask. "Does he have a name?"

"He calls himself Mr. Kramm. He gave Father gold, to lease our property. Father knew it was tainted, but gold it was. How, may I ask, are you acquainted with Mr. Kramm?"

"We met," I say. "Kind of a while back."

We're interrupted by a woman's voice that sounds very much like someone's mom.

"Elizabeth! Daniel! Come now, children! There be chores to do!"

"It's Mother!" Daniel says, alarmed. "We best be going . . . Mel. Mother has forbidden us to come here while the property's leased. It wouldn't do, she says, to poke our noses in others' affairs."

Elizabeth puts her hand on Daniel's arm. "Stay, brother," she says. "Stay for one minute more. Did you hear what he said? General Washington may be in danger. Is it not our duty to do what we can?"

"Mother will not be pleased," Daniel says. "Not in the slightest."

"But is she ever?" Elizabeth says.

"She is not," says Daniel. "But we must obey. Or else we incur her wrath."

"Listen," I say. "The last thing your mother would want—or your father—is for anything to happen to General Washington on your property. Think about that. And the fact your father took gold from—from Germans? That's not going to look good."

Daniel holds up his hand. "Let me talk with my sister,"

he says. "It will only be a moment." They walk a few yards away to discuss it. And they keep their voices low, so I can't overhear.

A minute goes by. Then another. Finally they walk back over. "It's settled," Daniel says. "We shall suffer Mother's wrath, yet again. Mel, you must prove to us that what you say is true. Or else we shall inform the Germans that you trespass upon their lease."

FORTY-THREE

THE THING I'M THINKING IS, *Man, I really need to know what time it is.* And if I take out my iPhone, turn it on, and check, it will spook Daniel and Elizabeth like no one's business. Nor do I see either of them wearing wristwatches, which I don't think have even been invented yet. So I'm going to have to guesstimate it: Ten-twenty? Ten-thirty?

It's going to matter. At exactly eleven I have to be in the stable in order to greet Brandon and Bev personally. I want to be the first person they see, so I can explain things to them.

"All right," I say. "Let me prove to you that what I'm saying is true. In what direction are Washington's troops headquartered?"

They both point to their right.

"Is that north?"

"It is," says Daniel.

"And where is the road to go north? Outside the farm?"

"The main road is about two miles beyond the farm," says Daniel. "From that, there's a smaller road that leads here."

"And how far is it to that smaller road?"

"It's just over there," says Elizabeth. "Past the trees on the left."

"And if someone comes down the road—when would you know about it?"

"Depending on the wind, we would know it when we hear it."

"Well, here's what's going to happen," I say. "Any minute now General Washington and this Mr. Kramm of yours are going to be coming down that road. General Washington thinks he's going to be inspecting a dozen prime horses. Mr. Kramm has other ideas. Our job is going to be to . . . to stop Mr. Kramm from . . . implementing any of his ideas. And protect General Washington. So your proof, Elizabeth, will be appearing any minute on the road."

It's my theory, and I'm sticking with it. I move past Daniel and Elizabeth and start heading out to the road, the one just past the trees on the left.

I figure if Daniel and Elizabeth are going to come,

they'll come. If they're going to heed their mother's call and go do chores—which is what must have happened the other time I was around—it would explain why they didn't notice Mr. Kramm and General Washington coming by and witness what was about to happen. Or what will happen. Or what was going to happen.

Whatever. It all somehow makes sense to me. I've trudged thirty yards, and haven't looked back. If I have to do it myself, I guess I can.

Then I hear Elizabeth call out. "Mel," she says. "You're going the wrong way. The road is over here. Have you no sense of direction? What do they teach you over there in New Jersey, if I may ask?"

Okay, so I was a little off. I turn around and see Daniel and Elizabeth, walking at a different angle toward the road. I run to catch up.

"Daniel! Elizabeth!" we hear their mother shout. "Come right now, children!"

"I did not hear a thing," says Elizabeth.

"Nor I," says Daniel.

"Me neither," I say. Two minutes later, we come to the road, and all of us stop and listen.

We hear the tramping of horses' hooves.

Then we see, in the distance, kicking up snow, horsemen coming our way.

"There be your proof," Daniel says to Elizabeth.

"My Lord," says Elizabeth, and her hand flies up to cover her mouth.

She is both shocked and awed. There is no mistaking the man coming up the road astride a majestic white horse: General George Washington.

Fully alive, I might add. And, at least for the moment, fully well.

FORTY-FOUR

GENERAL WASHINGTON INDEED.

Not only is he on every dollar bill in America, and in every car commercial on President's Day, but I've also seen him myself, not so long ago in the future. He was, at that time, dead as ye olde doornail, of course, but still. The guy's recognizable.

Big time.

There are four guys on horses, all abreast, coming our way. Four I recognize. General Washington, first off. He's a giant compared to the other guys. He sits tall in his saddle, almost like he's standing up. He has on black boots, buff breeches, a great blue coat, and an elaborate gold-trimmed black hat.

His horse, naturally, is the biggest of the bunch—a great, snorting white beast.

To the general's left is another military man—smaller than Washington, and riding a horse three-quarters the size of Washington's horse. Him, I've never seen, but I'm guessing he's some kind of aide-de-camp.

But the two guys to Washington's right?

Them, I've seen.

The last time I was here.

One of them is short, with a smashed-in face and a crooked nose. Who calls himself Mr. Kramm. He rides right next to General Washington, and his horse—a black beauty—is nearly as big as Washington's. He seems determined—*super* determined—to stay as close to the general as he possibly can. The other guy I've seen before rides on the outside. I've never heard him speak, this one, but I don't like him anyway.

They come down the road like they're in a hurry, trampling up snow, and maybe the last thing they expect to see is three *kids* along the side, trying to wave them down. Mr. Kramm doesn't appear to have any interest whatsoever in stopping to find out what we want. Nor does his comrade.

The aide-de-camp keeps his eyes straight ahead, as if he hasn't seen us. He's young, this guy—twenty, twenty-five tops. And definitely on the short side. He's maybe half as big as General Washington.

The general sees us waving our arms, hears us calling his name. He holds up his gloved right hand and pulls on the reins of his great white horse, and the company stops in the snow.

The horses snort. Steam pours from their muzzles.

"Children," says General Washington. He is five feet away, upon his steed, looking down. "Why have you hailed us?"

I am too awestruck to speak. First of all, this is *George Washington,* for crying out loud.

And second, he is alive.

So long as he lives, so lives the revolution.

"Children," he says again, this time impatiently. "What is it?" I see that he glances at my clothes and my Nikes but makes no remark.

I haven't thought of what to say, and the first thing that comes to my mind—*Hello there, General, I'm from the twenty-first century and I'm here to make sure you do not die today*—just won't do. I have to think of an alternative, and I have to be quick about it, but the thing is? He's a giant up there on his great white horse. And he doesn't seem pleased in the slightest.

Mr. Kramm intercedes. "*Mein* general," he says in his thick German accent. "Ve have not much time. The stable is not far." And then Mr. Kramm glares at me like he not only knows me from *before,* but knows exactly what I'm up to *now.*

It's eerie. Like, weird, even. This Mr. Kramm dude is *totally* staring me down. Then I notice, strapped to his shoulder, a leather satchel. On its side are big black letters: T.G.W., INC. Which is the same company that brought me the iTime app.

"Uh," I say. My first word to our first president—brilliant, no? "Um," I continue. "Mr. Presi—I mean General Washington?"

"Yes, boy?"

"Do you think we could have a word with you? In private? My friends here are Daniel and Elizabeth. Their father owns this farm. We think we have some information that you need to know. Privately." My eyes, in case he didn't get my drift, shift from him to the two German "farmers" to his right.

"Absolutely not!" says Mr. Kramm. "General, time is, as you told us yourself, of the essence. There is no time for—for—frivolous—children!"

The general silences Mr. Kramm with a withering glance. Then, to Daniel and Elizabeth: "'Tis true?" he says. "Your parents own this farm?"

"They do, sir," Daniel says. "They have leased it to Mr. Kramm. Most recently."

"Recently, you say? How recent?"

"Two weeks ago, sir. And from what we understand, Father was paid quite handsomely for the privilege."

General Washington glances at his aide-de-camp, silently sending him a communication. "Interesting," he says. Then: "Very well. You wish to discuss something with me in private. Gentlemen, if you would excuse us. Captain Powell," he says to his aide-de-camp. "Remain here with our friends." He then gives a tug on the reins of his white horse and moves twenty yards away.

The general brings his horse to a stop, crossways in the middle of the road. We go to the far side of the horse, which protects us from German "farmers" and any over-eager ears. I don't get the feeling that General Washington is merely indulging some kids for his amusement, or that he makes a practice of being hailed along the side of the road. I sense he is suspicious of something, and not necessarily of us.

"Go on," he says. His eyes shift, to make sure Kramm and his cohort haven't come any closer. "What is it you wish to tell me?"

"General Washington," I say. "If you've come for horses, there are none. The men you are with are not farmers, they are Hessian soldiers—worse than that, they are Hessian agents. Their mission is to kill you, which they are planning to do as soon as they get you in the horse stable. With your death, they believe, so will die the revolution."

"Do you two believe as he?" he asks Daniel and Elizabeth.

"It is a tale most incredulous," says Daniel. "But at our farmhouse, there are remaining Hessians. They have not a pretense, for farming or anything else. They are dressed in full Hessian uniform. My sister and I conferred, and thought it better to warn you than to not."

"I have," the general said, "such a desire for horses. . . . Captain Powell, who accompanies me, did give a fair warning—but a dozen horses! At fair prices! I'm afraid

I was lured. Have you proof of your charges? Though I already have suspicion enough that what you say is true. Threats upon my person are nothing new, and I have disregarded them all—to the dismay of my aides, no doubt. The one gentleman—Mr. Kramm, he calls himself—has more than a passing interest in things military. Indeed, he said he has been at this farm for nearly a year. Not a mere two weeks, as you attest. Both of you cannot be correct in the facts. And I believe the facts themselves shall be enough to allow us to settle the case.

"And if what you say proves true? Then I should think all of us would find ourselves in a fair bit of danger. Indeed, imminent danger would seem to be a distinct possibility. I shall have to play this careful . . ."

Unfortunately, there'll be no more time for care. Behind us, Mr. Kramm calmly takes his Luger from his coat, turns, and shoots the general's aide-de-camp, Captain Powell.

FORTY-FIVE

Captain Powell falls off his horse, the other horses neigh and jump, and General Washington, in that critical moment, calculates that his army now consists of two boys and one girl.

So he does what any other sane man would do. He bolts.

He whacks his great white horse on its flank, and it takes off.

Kramm and his partner whack their horses and take off after him.

No one—I mean no one—pays the slightest bit of attention to Daniel, to Elizabeth, or to me.

This all happens, by the way, in about five, maybe six seconds. From the shot to the whacks.

"My Lord," says Elizabeth. We rush over to Captain

Powell, who's been shot in the shoulder. Blood—a lot of it—is pouring down his chest, but he's able to sit up.

"Go!" he says. "Leave me! Help the general! There's a pistol in my pocket!"

"What about you?" I ask Captain Powell.

"I'll be fine, blast it!" He winces. "Now go! Take my horse and help him!"

Daniel pats around and pulls out of the Captain's coat a long black pistol. "One shot," Daniel says. "It's all we'll have."

"Let's make it count," I say, and then we catch Captain Powell's loose horse and all of us climb on. It takes some doing, and I'm by far the most inept, but all three of us manage to get aboard. Daniel has the reins, then Elizabeth, then me, and off we go.

The road inclines upward, and it takes us ninety seconds of hard slogging through snow to reach the apex. From here we can see the farmhouse below, the stable, and three or four other smaller buildings. What we can't see is General Washington, or any of his pursuers.

"What'll he do?" Daniel asks. "Has he a weapon?"

"I'm betting he doesn't," I say. "He's the general of an army, on a little side trip to purchase some horses. I don't think he would have bothered arming himself. I didn't see that he even had a sword."

"Then what?" says Elizabeth. "He can't just ride around through the snow. They'll hunt him down, like they would a fox."

"Could he try to get help?" I ask.

"From where?"

"How about your uncle?"

"Our uncle? How do you know about our uncle?"

"I don't know," I say. "I must have heard."

"Unless General Washington brought gold, he'll find no help from our uncle, I can assure you. It's going to be up to us, I'm afraid."

A few minutes later we see that the tracks diverge.

"They separated," Daniel says. "Like any hunter would in going after their prey. They'll try to find him and flush him out."

"And the general?" I say. "What would be his best strategy?"

"He needs to double back upon his own trail, if he can. Go in one direction, come back, go another. Try to confuse them, if he can. If he can't, they will just follow the track and come at him from different directions. Two against one. If they have experience, it should be simplicity itself."

"Should he get off his horse? Proceed on foot?"

"To what end? His feet still leave tracks. His only chance is to stay upon his horse, and hope for divine intervention."

"Or us," says Elizabeth. "We need to improve his odds."

"There's two of them, sister," says Daniel. "Likely armed."

"There are three of us," she says. "We have arms as

well, plus wits, plus knowledge. Surely we can do something."

Then we see to our right, riding at full gallop across naked farmland, Mr. Kramm.

"Swat him!" yells Daniel. "Upon his back flank—hard as you can!"

It takes me a beat to realize what he means. Then I do, and with my right hand I slap our horse, and yell, "Giddyup!"

Giddyup we do, though not nearly as fast as Mr. Kramm. But fast enough to throw the least experienced of us—that would be me—off the horse.

I fall with a thud. If it weren't for the snow, I might have broken something, like my tailbone.

Daniel and Elizabeth press on.

A minute passes.

Then another.

I can't hear or see. I don't know where anyone is or what is happening.

Until I hear something in the not-so-far distance: the unmistakable sound of a gunshot. It goes like this: *crack*. And the sound splits the sky.

Followed, nearly instantaneously, by a cry of pain. A gut-wrenching, hair-raising, blood-curdling scream, if you want a more precise description.

A man's scream, I'm certain, not a kid's. Which means not Daniel, and not Elizabeth.

Either one of the two Germans. Or the commander-in-chief of the Continental Army.

FORTY-SIX

I RUN ABOUT A HUNDRED yards through the snow, catch my bearings, and then run another hundred and turn left, where land ends and trees begin. General Washington, I'm thinking, unless he was just hit, would have headed for the woods. He probably figured his chances would be better there than in the open.

But he hasn't been hit. Down by the trees, I see Kramm's partner in the snow, holding his shoulder, and his horse bolting away.

And next to the man, in the white snow, a red pool of blood.

So he must have been shot in the same place Captain Powell was shot, which is only fair.

I keep running. Forward. Into harm's way.

"Mel!" I hear Daniel shout. "Get down!"

I get down. A shot, from my left, whizzes over my head.

I land in the snow, face first. I turn and see Kramm, on his big black horse, charging toward me. I am one dead duck.

He's coming at me with speed. I can almost feel the iron horseshoes—all four of them—trampling me.

Then, from the woods, I see a white flash.

General Washington's magnificent steed comes flying my way. Either he's going to intercept Kramm's horse, or he's going to run me over himself.

Both horses are maybe three feet away. Something so bad is about to happen to me I can't watch. I close my eyes and count: three.

Two.

One.

FORTY-SEVEN

THREE, TWO, ONE, *BAM*.

So this is it, I think. *This is what it's like. The pearly gates.*

I feel myself lifted up. White all around me. A special kind of white. Snow white.

Snow white? Lifted up?

The white I see *is* snow, and the lifting up is by the powerful left hand of General George Washington, who has plucked me off the ground a fraction of a second before I was going to be trampled to death by Kramm's angry black stallion.

As soon as Kramm sees Washington, he tries to get a shot off, but his Luger misfires. He tries again, and he misfires again. He yells something in German and rides off.

Then General Washington drops me, without ceremony, in another patch of snow twenty yards away. I'm pretty sure rescuing a kid wasn't on his to-do list today, and I try to thank him, but he waves me off.

Daniel and Elizabeth rush over to see if I'm all right, leading their horse behind them.

"My Lord!" she says. "Are you all right? Are you hurt?"

I'm not hurt, and I am all right. She helps me get to my feet, and then Daniel sees something.

"He's going back to the farmhouse!" Daniel says. "He'll get reinforcements!"

We watch Kramm gallop across the field. General Washington pulls up beside us. "That man"—he nods over his shoulder—"is hit. Who shot him?"

"I shot him, sir," Daniel says. "With Captain Powell's pistol."

"Captain Powell," General Washington says. "He's alive?"

"He is. He was shot in the shoulder, same as that one. If neither loses too much blood, I suspect both will live."

"We will make sure of Captain Powell, at least. He did warn me. And Kramm?" General Washington asks, nodding toward the farmhouse. "Where to for him?"

"To the farmhouse," Daniel says. "There are two, at least, uniformed men there. They have weapons"

"Have they horses?"

"Just the ones they rode in on, sir."

"We have two," the general says. "He has one. Where's the other? Scattered?"

"I believe so, sir," says Daniel.

"Can it be called?"

"By the Hessians? I do not know. It will likely return to the stable, however."

The stable . . . the stable . . . the stable . . . oh no.

"What time is it?" I ask.

No one has a watch, but the general states the obvious. "It is morning, young man," he says. "Almost noon, I should say. Have you someplace else to go?"

"The stable!" I say. "I have to be there right now! It's urgent!"

"Urgent?" asks General Washington. "What could be urgent in a stable?"

"I'll tell you when we get there," I say, and General Washington lifts me onto his mount. Daniel and Elizabeth climb aboard the other horse, and five minutes later we are at the stable. Along the way I sneak a peek at my iPhone: as we arrive, it's ten-fifty-eight. Which gives me two whole minutes to explain absolutely everything to the Father of Our Country.

FORTY-EIGHT

I TRY MY BEST. "GENERAL Washington," I say. "We're about to see something, and all I have time to say about it is this: do you believe in miracles?"

"I am afraid, young man, that I do not."

Elizabeth seems even more skeptical than General Washington—she's acting like she expects me to show her a magic trick. Which probably isn't far from the truth.

"Well," I say, "hold on to your hats, folks. Because I think in about thirty seconds or so you're going to see something you're going to have a hard time believing."

We're in the stable. There are no horses inside, but there are the stacks of hay, the saddles hanging up on a wall, the bunches of rope, and the by now all-too-familiar god-awful stench.

The seconds tick down. My iPhone is on.

And it starts to buzz.

It starts to shake, rattle, and roll.

It starts to tweet and toot and whistle.

And then before us, as if emerging from a mist, come Bev and Brandon.

Brandon's wearing sneakers, jeans, and his red hat. The one that has a picture of a snarling wolf—I mean a snarling *lobo*—on it. Bev has on her pink jacket, and she's wearing her earmuffs. Both of them are clutching their iPhones, which are blinking and buzzing like crazy.

Bev and Brandon jump back as if electrified.

General Washington, Daniel, and Elizabeth jump back as if horsewhipped.

There's a standoff. Between the eighteenth and twenty-first centuries.

I step into the breach.

"General Washington," I say. "May I present to you my esteemed classmates, who visit us from another land: Miss Beverly, and Master Brandon. Everybody, say hello."

"What land is this?" says General Washington.

"New Jersey," I say. "Just across the river."

It's Bev who has the most presence of mind. She takes note of me, Daniel, and Elizabeth, and then General George Washington. Bev smiles, like she gets the whole thing.

"Why, General Washington," she says, and curtsies. "How very pleased we are to meet you."

I did say *curtsies*. And a very well-executed one, I must

say. I didn't know she had it in her, but then again, no matter how hard she tries to hide it, Bev's got more than a little of her mom's actress gene in her blood. She extends her hand.

General Washington has no choice—being a gentleman, born and bred—but to step forward and take her hand. "As am I," he says. "Though these circumstances are most peculiar. I should like to have a word with your parents."

"My mother is in California," says Bev. "In a play."

"Dude," says Brandon. "Like, my mom's out west, but you're one heck of a realistic reenactor. Man, this is one great show! And I thought I had hit the wrong button or something on my phone and was going to be in for it. It's all part of the setup, isn't it?" Then Brandon holds out his fist. "Pound me, brother!"

General Washington does not, alas, fist bump Brandon. He frowns instead, as if the impertinence is beyond the pale. "Why does your . . . your hat . . . have a picture upon it? Is it a wolf? What is the explanation for this?"

"It's a *lobo,* man. It means 'wolf.' In Spanish. It brings us luck."

"It brings *who* luck?"

"New Mexico."

"What need does a distant territory have for luck?"

"He's joking, right?" Brandon asks me.

"I don't think he is," I say, but by now it's obvious the general is not pleased.

"How can it be," he says, "that you all . . . appeared,

if you will . . . out of nothing more than thin air? Is this some kind of parlor trick? At a time such as this?"

"Well, General," I start to explain. "Let me put it like this. We are friends of yours. The kind of friends you may not be used to, but maybe the very best friends you could ever have. We kind of know stuff that nobody else has a way of knowing. Which is why we stopped you in the road. And if we hadn't? It's quite possible that they would have shot you dead, right here in one of the stalls. And the implications of that, sir, are quite enormous. The word would spread like wildfire. And without you, the Continental Army might become nothing more than a savage band of pillagers looting their way through the countryside."

"Oh man," says Brandon. "Don't be such a downer, dude! It's only playacting!"

"I demand to know," says General Washington, drawing himself up to his full height, "what exactly is going on at this moment. Do you take me for a fool, lad? You bring me to this stable and then you conjure up"—he gestures dismissively at Bev and Brandon—"these—these—court jesters? Dressed in—these costumes, and each of them holding—what is it they are holding? And you as well? What is that infernal contraption in your hands? I demand answers!"

FORTY-NINE

IT WOULD BE NICE to explain everything to both sides—the eighteenth-century people and the twenty-first-century people—and have them understand, accept, agree, move forward—but A) that's not happening anytime soon, and B) remember the German dudes—Kramm, and the two Hessian soldiers back at the farmhouse? Funny thing is, they haven't forgotten about us. Or rather, they haven't forgotten about General Washington. And now they've got him right where they want him, which is in the horse stable, where they intended to kill him in the first place.

They've taken up positions. One soldier is at each end of the stable, ready to shoot any of us who try to get out.

And Kramm is holding, high above his head, a flaming torch.

Bev and Brandon still think this is some kind of *re-enactment*.

Daniel and Elizabeth are properly horrified, but General Washington?

He's mad.

As mad as I've ever seen a man. Madder than I've ever seen my father get, and that's saying something, because Dad's got that volcanic, shouting temper thing, which I truly hate. His face contorts, turns red, his lips twist into a growling grimace, and out it flies.

The general's anger takes a different form. His face is stone-cold set. I don't think you could pry his lips apart if you had a crowbar. And his eyes are black with fury.

And you know who he's mad at? He's mad at *us*. For leading him *here*. Which, he soon tells us, is completely *indefensible*.

"I shall shoot myself, should they not," General Washington says, "for allowing myself to be led by a bunch of *children* into this position. My second great mistake in one day!"

Mr. Kramm touches the torch to the roof on the right side.

Then he torches the bottom of the wall on the left side.

Now it's just a matter of you know what.

Time.

FIFTY

"Why," says Brandon, "are those reenactor dudes, like, torching the place? What's up with *that*?"

"Boys," says Bev. "I think we need to think of something. Now would be a very good time."

"Silence!" commands General Washington. "I must think. Your constant babbling is of no help!"

The general is the kind of guy you pay attention to, so we shut up. Under his hat his hair is turning gray, but it isn't as white as you might think. I know he never wore a wig. Around this time he's in his forties, if I'm not mistaken, though his hat and his uniform make him appear, at a distance, a lot older, like in his late fifties or even early sixties.

But he is younger. You can tell by his face: relatively

wrinkle-free. The wrinkles he will have in the future are being created as we speak.

And I know what you're thinking: what's the deal with the dude's teeth?

Well, let me tell you: they are not, contrary to popular belief, made of wood.

Not to say they appear completely natural. They're kind of oversized, maybe, sort of like a pair of too-big dentures, but they are definitely not made from wood. Maybe some other more toothlike substance—mother-of-pearl, or whalebone—but for sure not wood, or real teeth.

At the moment, he doesn't seem overly self-conscious about his teeth, real or unreal. At the moment, he seems more rightly concerned about the fact that the roof of the stable is aflame, as is the wall at the left corner. Both fires are on a flight path to meet in the middle, and the whole dang thing is going to come tumbling down.

So I get the basic idea: burn down the stable, make us run out, shoot us dead.

The thing is? It doesn't happen exactly *instantly*.

Fire's funny, like it has a mind of its own. The stable is completely made of wood, and there's hay everywhere, but it takes a while for the fire to decide to get really going. Which gives us time to contemplate our situation.

It's not good. And every time we try to think of something together, General Washington tells us to be silent.

Which doesn't sit so well with Bev.

"Listen, mister," Bev says, and puts her hands on her hips. "Have you noticed that it's getting a little warm in here? You want us to just stand around until you think of something to do?"

"Bev," I say. "This is *General* Washington, remember."

"Yeah?" she says. "So what's your point?"

"Be silent!" General Washington says, with a little less conviction than before. I think the problem is that he doesn't know what to do any more than we do.

"Well, I for one am not just going to stand here. Who *are* those people, for one thing? And two, what do they want? Mel? Is this totally crazy or what?"

We start to argue. Which isn't cool, you know, to be arguing among ourselves right in front of George Washington, but this fire thing is really starting to pick up.

And whatever time we might have had to devise a plan is, uh, up in smoke.

The fires meet in the middle, and we run out right before part of the roof falls on top of us. And I mean *run.* You might be surprised by how every single cell in your body screams at you with one simple instruction: run! Run now, as fast as you can!

So we run, even though I am fully expecting Kramm and his men to have their muskets loaded and ready, and to shoot to kill.

The thing is, I feel kind of *responsible* here. I shouldn't just be worried about saving my own skin, should I?

What should I do about General Washington? About Daniel and Elizabeth? About Brandon and Bev?

Fire and flame; the colors orange and red, leaping from white snow; smells of smoke, burning planks, and horse manure; sounds of crackling timber, falling roof beams; the taste of charred wood upon our lips and tongues; and pure dumb, blind fear in the pits of our stomachs as we exit the stable and face another kind of fire.

I can't see anyone else at first. Though I hear horses neighing.

I've lost everyone, and I don't know how to find them. Then I hear the crack of musket fire—seven, eight, ten shots.

I throw myself into the snow to avoid musket balls and to put out whatever flames might have gotten me.

I look up.

Elizabeth and Brandon, who barely know each other, who met, like, what, *two minutes* ago, are holding on to each other like they're long-lost lovers.

And while I'm trying to process *that*, I see before us a ring of soldiers on horseback, loading and firing their muskets, and then loading and firing them again.

Soldiers from the Continental Army of these United States.

Propped on one horse, with his shoulder in a make-shift bandage, is the general's aide, Captain Powell, who seems to be in charge.

"The cavalry," says Brandon, "has come to save us. Huzzah, right?"

Not right, I think, getting to my feet. *Where's General Washington?*

Daniel?

Bev?

Nothing will be completely right unless I find all of them alive and well.

FIFTY-ONE

I TURN, MAKE A MOVE to run back to the stable, but I'm restrained.

Physically.

By Continental soldiers.

"You'll not be going there, lads and lassie," says a guy who has grabbed me by the collar. "You'll be in the crossfire. Let us conclude our business, and then we'll sort things out."

"My brother's in there!" cries Elizabeth.

"Bev is in there!" cries Brandon.

"General Washington is in there!" I cry.

"And we'll get them all out," the soldier says. Then, to himself, perhaps more grimly than he intends: "One way or another."

Elizabeth breaks free. Daniel has not yet emerged from the flames.

As she runs toward the burning barn, the soldier holding me by the collar loosens his grip, and I break free as well. I'm more worried about Elizabeth getting shot by one of the Continental soldiers on horseback than I am of her running into fire in search of Daniel.

She runs, I run, two soldiers behind us run after us. Brandon stays put. He's still trying to figure things out. Maybe he thinks this is still part of some *reenactment*.

Before things get hairy, we are stopped. People, our people, are emerging from the smoking ruins.

"Elizabeth!" I hear Daniel say, before I can see him. "I am not harmed, nor is she!"

Bev emerges next, and she is not only peeved, she is *monumentally* peeved. Embers of burning wood have fallen on her spiffy jacket, her boots are dirty, and, worst of all, some junky stuff has gotten into her *hair.*

But none of that is what's gotten Bev ticked off. "I've had it with that guy!" Bev says. "Who the heck does he think he is?

"That's General Washington, Bev—is he all right?"

"Ask him yourself," Bev says. "And tell him that the next time he tells me to be silent, I'm going to kick him in the shins!"

FIFTY-TWO

THERE'S MORE FIRE NOW in the stable, less smoke—the place is really going up. Then I see a fiery blur, from the far right side of the structure. General George Washington, hatless, hair charred, eyes blazing, emerges from the fire, and walks straight over to Bev and me. "I demand answers!" General Washington says. "Who are you people, in such costume? Have you conspired to kill me? Answer now, or I swear I shall have you hanged!"

I wish I could give him an easy answer. But talking to General Washington when he's steaming mad and his hair is smoking and his eyes are blazing is positively *scary*. So I say: "Well, General, it's a . . . um . . . ah . . . er . . ."

Bev, naturally, isn't so easily cowed. "You see here," she says. "You have no business talking to us like that!"

General Washington and Bev, I'm beginning to sense, are not going to be best pals anytime soon. General Washington literally grits his teeth—his *fake* teeth, that is—like he almost can't stop himself from saying something really foul to Bev. But she's just a kid, right? And a girl. So whatever he was thinking of saying, he doesn't.

Instead he looks at our hands. At what we're holding in our hands. And that sets him off on a brand-new topic.

"What," he says, "are those . . . boxes? Why are you holding them thusly?"

Brandon walks up and says, "It's a phone, dude. Whaddya think it is? And you better put your hair out, 'cause it's going to, like, light up any minute now."

This is not really the proper way to address General George Washington.

This does not go over well.

The general pats his hair down, to put out any fires, and then I think he's just about ready to smite Brandon with the back of his hand when one of the Continental soldiers comes up to him. "Two dead, Excellency," he says. "Two Hessian soldiers."

"Only two?" I say. "What happened to the other one? The guy holding the torch?"

General Washington redirects his wrath from Brandon to me. "Silence!" he says. "You will not speak unless spoken to!" Then he turns to the soldier and says, "And what of the other? The one who held the torch?"

"That's Kramm," I say. "He must be found, General Washington! At all costs!"

"I said, silence!" General Washington explodes. "Another word and I'll have your tongue! Find him," he says to the soldier. "And bring him to me. He shall be questioned. And then he shall be hanged."

FIFTY-THREE

BEV AND BRANDON, I see, are about to short-circuit.

I can't blame them. The last fifteen minutes have been kind of on the hairy side. And before that, the only thing they had to worry about was getting through the Christmas dinner the school was going to have for us.

I grab both of them by the arm and tug them away. I figure all I need is a few minutes to explain things.

Bev's angry, and Brandon's confused. They start asking questions at the same time. They pipe down for a half second to give me a chance to answer, but then they start right in again. I put my hands up and out in protest. "Let me explain!" I say. "Will you all just shut up, please, so I can tell you what's what?"

Finally they do. "All right," says Bev. "You seem to

know so much, Mel. What's going on? You know how much trouble we're in? I'm telling you, they might use this as an excuse to throw us out of school!"

"Let me explain," I say. "Now, do you remember, back in the basement of the Taylorsville General Store? Brandon was fooling around with a MacBook?"

"Of course we remember," Bev says. "That was, like, fifteen minutes ago."

"Well, for you, maybe it was fifteen minutes ago, but not for me."

"You're losing me, dude," says Brandon. "Fifteen minutes is fifteen minutes."

"Sometimes it isn't," I say. "If you remember, Brandon was fooling around with this MacBook, and then our iPhones started going haywire. It was because we were all downloading a new app. It's called iTime. And believe it or not, it zapped us back here. Which is *not* a reenactment. This is the real deal, guys. It actually *is* Christmas Day, 1776. And that guy you were just yelling at, Brandon? He's no reenactor. He's General George Washington himself. And one thing he has never seen in his life is an iPhone, which is why he was asking you about it."

Brandon blinks.

So does Bev.

Then Brandon snaps his fingers. "I get it—we traveled back in time! Now it all fits! I was trying to talk to one of those soldier dudes and, like, he really smelled! I was thinking, Man, these reenactor dudes really put a lot of effort into, you know, making themselves seem realistic! But they're not reenactors—they're real Continental Army dudes! How cool is that?"

"Get out of here, Brandon," says Bev. "There's no such thing as time travel. This is a massive screwup. A Revolutionary War reenactment that went way, way wrong. There's going to be lawsuits, Mel. When my mother finds out about this, watch out."

"If my mother finds out," Brandon says, "she'll think it's totally cool. She'll think maybe I should stick around."

"Boys," says Bev. "Let's think this through here. Mel—if what you say is true—and I'm not sure what's true and what isn't at this point—then the question is, how do we get out of here? Back to where we belong?"

"It's simple," I say. "It's what I've been trying to tell you—I've figured it out. I was here before—the same time, really—but things happened differently. Washington was actually shot and killed. And you guys were taken prisoner by the Hessians. So I went to Philadelphia and with Dr. Franklin's help recharged my iPhone and then we figured out this iTime app. All we have to do is reprogram it. And it will put us right back where we belong."

"Dr. Franklin?" says Brandon. "Who's Dr. Franklin?"

"Benjamin Franklin," I say. "You know: *the* Benjamin Franklin. Now check your phone, and you'll see the app I'm telling you about. iTime. It wasn't there before, but it's there now."

Sure enough, we all have the app called iTime. We press the icons, and we get the same messages as before.

Welcome to iTime.
Brought to You by T.G.W., Inc.
The Aim Is to Play.
To Mess About.
Who Says Things Have to Be This Way and Not Another?
Who Says Things Wouldn't Be Better if a Different Road Had Been Taken?
Catch Us if You Can.
K.

We read this, and as we do the message fizzles away and disappears. A new screen appears. Five large boxes with a place to put the day, the month, the year, the time, and the place.

All this is just like last time. Except now I know exactly what to do. I'm about to have us all reprogram our phones to bring us home—to bring us to *our* time, that is—when a phalanx of Continental soldiers surrounds us.

"Arrest them!" yells General Washington, pointing an accusatory finger at us, then at Daniel and Elizabeth. "Arrest all of these infernal children! And confiscate those—those—those boxes they hold in their hands!"

FIFTY-FOUR

STRONG, ROUGH HANDS GRAB us by the neck and shoulders. The hand around my own neck is big. The guy could, if he wanted, choke me to death with just a smidgen more pressure.

Bev hisses and says, "Keep your hands off me," to no avail.

Brandon says, "Yo, easy, dudes."

Daniel and Elizabeth fare no better. They are grabbed separately and bound together; no one listens when they shout that they live on this farm and their parents are expecting them back right this minute.

And they have taken our iPhones. In my case, with one giant hand around my throat and one holding my upper left arm, there isn't much I can do about it. Same with the others. The guys who grabbed our phones pass them along to the next guys, like a bucket drill, and they are then passed up the line, and finally given to a very short officer who stands next to General Washington.

"This I say once and once only," the general begins. He is not talking to us at the moment, but rather to his men. Besides the officer next to him, who has our iPhones, there aren't that many regular soldiers—a dozen perhaps. They must have been ordered to follow the general as he went about his horse-purchasing operation, just in case.

"I repeat," says General Washington. "I shall say this once and once only: none of you shall ever speak of this day. None of you shall ever mention, in your tents to your comrades, or in letters home, or in idle chat to common passersby, anything at all about the events that have transpired on this farm. Never! Posterity must not know, and shall not know, a single word about any of this *whatsoever*. The penalty for violating this injunction shall be immediate death by firing squad. Do I make myself clear? Not—one—single—word—ever!" The general holds up his right forefinger and points at each man as he looks him in the eye.

There are no dissenters.

Each soldier gulps as the general stares him down.

Then Washington turns to the officer beside him— the short man who is now in possession of our phones. "Captain Hamilton," he says. "I want these children brought back to camp. I care not if they have parents or guardians—they have inserted themselves most obstreperously into a military campaign and therefore they shall abide by military rules. They shall be interrogated one by one. If we find evidence of espionage, treachery, or traitorous actions of any kind, they shall be executed. By the rope." He then walks over to our group. He points a long, thick finger at my nose. "We shall start with this one," he says. "Observe the iron on his teeth. One lie from him and he shall hang before midnight."

We are bound and blindfolded; then they hoist each of us upon a horse. Not solo, of course, but behind a soldier. Our hands are bound in front of us, not behind, so at least we can try to hold on. We gallop away; if any of us falls off, I suspect they'll just leave us, and consider any damage our due.

It's hard to tell how long we ride—a half hour, maybe longer—but finally we stop. They haul us off our horses, then remove our blindfolds and the ropes around our wrists.

Before us is a rather stately pale-yellow mansion. General Washington and Captain Hamilton are on the front steps of the house, conferring with a group of officers.

"'Tis the general's headquarters," Daniel whispers. "The finest house within twenty miles."

"Nothing but the best," I say. We are led inside. The ceilings are low and the floors are wood, but there are paintings on the walls, and one room is even set for tea. All of which tells us that we have entered, comparatively speaking, the heights of luxury. But none of it is for us.

Upstairs, where they take us, is even fancier. What

were bedrooms weeks before are now command centers: maps are spread upon tables, officers huddle around speaking in low murmurs, notes are being jotted down with quill pens. In the back is a very small room, with two very small beds, and into it we are shoved, all five of us, and the door is shut behind us.

Five voices talk at once. No one can possibly understand what anyone else is saying. Then the door to the room is opened and an angry officer tells us to shut up, and then he slams the door.

No one except me does.

The door is opened again, and this time the officer scowls. Then he points a finger at me and says: "You. Come now." He waits until I step forward, grabs my shoulder, and slams the door behind me.

"The general wants a word," he says. "By the by, the general's mood is most foul. If you value your neck, you'd best make double sure every word you give him be true."

We walk to the end of the hall, where two soldiers stand guard outside a closed door.

My escort knocks twice. The door is opened, and he shoves me in.

FIFTY-FIVE

GENERAL GEORGE WASHINGTON IS sitting regally behind a large oak desk. There's nothing on the desk except a map, a piece of paper, a quill pen, and an inkwell. And three iPhones, lined up very neatly.

Two black, one white.

Standing next to General Washington is the officer who was at the farm, Captain Hamilton, and another officer, who seems to be his superior. Captain Hamilton is short, and young, like, maybe twenty years old. He acts like he thinks he's hot stuff and knows it all. Then it hits me: the dude isn't just some guy named Hamilton. He's *Alexander* Hamilton. If everything works out the way's it's supposed to, he's going to get his face plastered on every ten-dollar bill in America. If I had my iPhone, I'd take his picture.

The other officer is older, maybe thirty-five at the max. I'm getting the impression he wouldn't mind hanging me then and there. His eyes are black, and burning. And even kind of *accusing*, like I'm to blame for something. *Dude,* I'd like to say. *What's your problem?*

There are no chairs in front of General Washington's desk. I'm guessing this is the way the dude rolls. *I am the commander; you are not. I sit. You do not.*

"Any and all discussions in this room," General Washington begins, "are entirely and completely private, and shall never be spoken of outside this room. With me are General Greene and Captain Hamilton. They can vouch for what I say. One violation, and you will be shot. There will be no jury or appeal. Do you understand?"

"I do," I say. "Sir."

"The proper form of address," interjects General Greene, "when speaking to General Washington is 'Your Excellency.'"

"It is?" I say. That seems weird to me, and somehow, dare I say it, un-American. *Your Excellency?*

"It most certainly is," General Greene says.

"Okay," I say. "If you say so."

"What is your name?" General Washington continues.

"My name is Mel," I tell him. "Your Excellency."

"Mel what?" I tell him my real full name.

"Your age?"

"Twelve."

"Your place of residence?"

"Fredericksville, New Jersey. That's where I go to school, anyway."

"You claimed this morning that Hessians aimed to kill me and alter the progress of the revolution, did you not?"

"I did. Sir. I mean, Your Excellency."

"And how did you come to have this knowledge?"

"Well, it's kind of a long story. Sir. Your Excellency. I could tell you one hundred percent of the truth, sir, but I have a feeling you might not believe me. But I won't lie. I would never tell a lie. Your Excellency, sir."

General Washington—believe it or not—kind of shakes his shoulders and rolls his eyes. "Those very words," he says, "give me pause. When someone tells me they would never tell a lie, I always make sure to have a firm grip upon my purse. Dispense with the tired homilies, young man. Tell me plainly how you came to know the Germans were soldiers, not farmers. And be quick about it. We haven't all day."

So much for the "I would never tell a lie" trick. I never believed that story about Washington, anyway. "All right," I said. "I know because . . . well, I guess you could say I saw it for myself."

"Saw what for yourself?"

"Your death, sir. I mean, Your Excellency."

"In a vision? A dream?"

"Nope. The real thing. You were dead, shot in the chest. In that horse stable. And that would mean no crossing the Delaware, no victory at Trenton, the revolution would fail, and there'd be no United States of America. Which would really stink. So I figured the best thing to do would be to go back in time one hour before that and fix it. With Dr. Franklin's help, that's sort of what happened."

General Washington keeps his eyes on mine the entire time I speak without shaking his head, or objecting, or laughing out loud, or pounding the table and telling me to shut up. He listens carefully, and displays no emotion.

"He's obviously quite mad, Excellency," says General Greene. "I believe his position is that he is from posterity. Shall I see him out?"

"You shall not, General Greene. If the young gentleman wishes to believe he is from posterity, we shall allow it. But his information is incorrect. There will be no crossing of the Delaware tonight, and therefore no attack upon the Hessians tomorrow in Trenton. The attack has been canceled, upon my orders, mere minutes ago. My forecasters predict snow and sleet, which makes any crossing tonight quite impossible. And if you—a twelve-year-old boy from New Jersey—know of my plans, I fear the entire enterprise is doomed. I therefore have called it off. No crossing. No attack. We shall soon inform the men. Perhaps you, young man, will be kind enough to inform posterity on our behalf, and tell them we poor mortals shall have to make the best of it. Send our regrets. But we act for ourselves first and posterity second. The weather is inclement; the enemy has no doubt been fore-warned. There will be no crossing tonight."

"You must!" I say, but I have been dismissed. Captain Hamilton takes me by the arm and leads me away.

Or tries to. They won't get rid of me without a fight.

TO THE LONGBOATS

FIFTY-SIX

"GENERAL WASHINGTON," I SAY, and I stand up as tall as I can. "You are not only wrong, you are dead wrong. You either cross the Delaware tonight and attack Trenton in the morning, or this revolution is over right here and now. Your men are itching to fight. They have a week left to their enlistment. You've been pushed out of New York and across New Jersey and you have nothing to show for it. You either fight now, or you lose now. There's no other choice."

"The—the—the impertinence!" sputters General Greene. "The—the audacity! A mere child—talking in such a manner to the commander in chief of the Continental Army!"

"And you, General Greene," I say, "always agree with every word General Washington says. Don't you?"

He stops midtirade, and a sheepish acknowledgement crosses his face. "We are a unified command," he says stiffly. "General Washington has made his decision and it is our responsibility to fulfill it to the very best of our abilities."

"It's the wrong decision," I say. "And you know it. It's tonight or never. The Hessians are in Trenton. The last thing they'll expect is an attack. Even if they have spies and have been told, they won't believe it. Today is Christmas Day. Who would ever think anyone would be crazy enough to cross the Delaware on Christmas Day? It's a brilliant plan, General Washington. It will be remembered throughout history. You've got to go through with it. You can't falter."

"History?" General Washington says. "What will they remember? That an obscure Virginian, a gentleman farmer, not a professional British soldier, led twenty-four hundred men to their doom? I know what the British think of me. I petitioned them, when I was a young man. I begged to be accepted into the officer corps of His Majesty's Army, and they refused me. I was a *colonialist*, not a proper Englishman. They scorned me then, and they scorn me now. They say I am an *amateur*. A rank amateur with desperate schemes. The weather is turning, young man. There is ice forming in the river. A storm is very nearly upon us. How shall we cross with twenty-four hundred men? And march them nine miles south? The idea is preposterous, utterly preposterous. It shames me to think I ever entertained it."

"Wow," I say. "I didn't think you'd give in so easily. It's not what the history books say about you. They say you are the 'indispensable man.' That without your determination and forbearance, and your ability to overcome any and all obstacles, there never would have been such a thing as the United States of America. You become our first president, sir. Our capital was established in your name. It's called Washington, D.C. It is a shining city upon a hill. And the monument to you is the tallest building in the entire city."

"By God," General Washington says, and a faraway gleam comes across his eyes. "I like it! Washington, D.C." Then his eyes flash. "Those, sir, are not my initials! I am 'Washington, G.' G., and only G. Who is this Washington, D.C., you speak of? I have no relations with such initials. What abomination is this? After all I have suffered? All I have risked? To be—to be insulted! In such a manner! 'Tis an outrage!"

"Your Excellency—if I may," General Greene says gently, soothingly. "He's a mere boy. He harbors delusions, I fear. He's not from posterity, sir—he's from *New Jersey*. What should one expect? I say we send him back with the others and think no more of any of them or what he said. It's complete tosh."

"General, if I may explain?" I say. "The *D.C.* is not anyone's initials. They stand for District of Columbia, as our nation is often called Columbia. The city of Washington, in the District of Columbia, lies along the Potomac River, a few miles from your home at Mount Vernon. Millions

225

of Americans go there every year to pay homage to the Father of Our Country. That's how you are known. Or will be known. Once you get your men across the river and defeat the Hessians tomorrow at Trenton."

"Oh," says General Washington. A smile crosses his face but is very quickly withdrawn. He coughs, and marches a piece of paper from the left side of his desk to the right. The silence is painfully uncomfortable. Captain Hamilton, standing behind the general, puts his hands out: it's all right, he seems to be saying. Give the guy a second.

We do. "Well then," General Washington finally says. "Perhaps I spoke too soon. I withdraw my remarks, and beg your indulgence."

"The boy is touched, Your Excellency, I swear an oath," says General Greene. "He speaks gibberish, and nothing but. I shall send him away at once."

General Washington holds up a hand. "Wait," he says. "This *District of Columbia*, you speak of. On the Potomac, you say? Within distance of Mount Vernon? I daresay it is a suitable place for a capital city—perhaps a bit far for John Adams and the Massachusetts men, but still, altogether suitable. And, young man, you refer to a 'president.' What position is this, precisely? President of what? How does it come to be established?" General Washington steeples his fingers, and his eyes regain their faraway gleam.

"It's what we call the leader of our country," I say.

"Which is to come. There will be a Constitutional Convention, in 1787, and all of this will be figured out when the Constitution is written. It establishes the United States of America."

"That," says Captain Hamilton, "is an estimable idea. What we have now is no country. We have thirteen squabbling colonies. They can't so much as raise a farthing to pay our men, though their lives depend upon it."

"General," says General Greene. "I beg you to dismiss this young man. He is obviously quite ill. You said yourself, not ten minutes ago, that attempting to cross the river this night is hopeless, utterly hopeless. You will not put the men to it."

"And did you not, General Greene, dispute my thoughts? Did you not make much the same argument this young man just made? If he be so ill, General Greene, what then about you?"

"I am a military officer, Your Excellency," General Greene says, not a little stiffly. "I gave you my professional judgment. This boy is ill and possessed by the devil, I fear. I beg you again not to give a second's pause to a word he says."

"You, General Greene, were, less than a year ago, a Quaker and a farmer with no land. Let us not puff up each other's military credentials, my good sir. We save that for the enemy, who disdain us, and for the men, who only partly disdain us. Thus far, that is. Ill this young man may be, but of the men he speaks the truth: if we shall not fight, we shall lose them all. Would not these horrid conditions in fact be our greatest asset? The bold stroke, General Greene—how I have advocated the bold stroke! What else have we? I am chagrined, sir. That I have been led around by the forecasters of weather and gloom. Perhaps I need to rethink the possibilities. Think of posterity, General Greene. Think of a shining city upon a hill. Posterity has sent us, by our great good fortune, this emissary who stands before us now."

"Sir, I beg you. The boy is a liar and a fool. Not posterity's emissary."

"Are you for a crossing, General Greene? You were. Are you not still?"

"I am indeed, sir. But for our own good reasons. Not predicated on the ravings of a lunatic. The boy is a fool, sir, I say again. No emissary is he."

"Are you quite sure of that, General Greene?"

"Of course I am, sir. It's ... preposterous to think otherwise."

"Then what, pray tell, be these?" General Washington says, and holds up one of the iPhones laid on his desk. "A most curious device, would you not say? And not of our own world, an unprejudiced mind could easily conclude. Not of our own world at all. Why not, General Greene, from another time? Another place?

"Time does not favor us. Nor does weather. If you notice, providence has chosen to make this day most inclement, but, upon reflection, I have decided it is a signal to proceed, rather than to falter. The higher the obstacle, the more gratifying the triumph.

"Let them go," General Washington says. "Let these children go. This one, and the others. They may have their devices back, I care not for them. General Greene—we have a river to cross, and we must begin preparations at once. Everyone to McKonkey's Ferry on the double-quick. We must inform the officers and then the men—time is wasting. We are about to give the enemy a capital strike, and he shan't ever forget that on this day, Christmas Day, free men of courage crossed a river of ice in the name of independence from tyranny. To the longboats, gentlemen. Our destiny awaits."

FIFTY-SEVEN

W<small>E'RE THROWN BACK INTO</small> the little bedroom and told to get ready. Everyone is clearing out in half an hour. It's about two o'clock in the afternoon. We're brought bread, and something one might call soup. And we're told we're leaving when they leave, whether we like it or not.

Other than that, we're pretty much left alone. Which means, when it comes down to it, that we're pretty much at each other's throats.

Nobody can agree on anything. Except maybe that I'm mostly to blame, just because.

Brandon and Bev want to go—meaning, back to the Fredericksville School. In the twenty-first century.

Daniel and Elizabeth, on the other hand, want to get

back to their farmhouse. Their horse stable is burned to the ground, for one thing. And if Kramm's Hessian friends are still around, they'll cause nothing but more trouble.

And me? Something is nagging at me. Something that feels . . . unfinished. I'm not sure what it is, but I do know that leaving the scene now doesn't feel right. So I do what I always do when I don't know what to do: I take out my iPhone and turn it on.

I have a bunch of texts from Mr. Hart. They've been sitting there unanswered since he sent them three hours ago. Or 240-odd years in the future, depending on how you think about it.

"Hold on," I say. "I have texts from Mr. Hart." I read them aloud.

Where R U? says the first one.

R U OK? says the second one.

R U together? says the third one.

Has anything . . . unusual happened? says the last one.

I have to keep in mind that *this* Mr. Hart is not exactly the *same* Mr. Hart that I was texting with before. The time before that time. Because I came back an hour earlier, remember? So this "Mr. Hart" texting me now is the same guy, but then again not quite exactly the same guy.

Get it? Good.

I type back: *We're OK. Ready to come back.*

We wait. Then the old micro three-chord signifying incoming.

R U sure nothing unusual has happened?

That's when it hits me. Maybe I should have known before now, but to tell you the truth, I hadn't thought it through.

But now—now I think I'm starting to figure some things out. Mr. Hart knows a good deal more than he's letting on. And you know what?

That doesn't sit well with me.

Kind of ticks me off.

What are we—*guinea pigs* or something?

"He knows," I say. "Mr. Hart."

"What a minute," says Bev. "You're telling me that you're getting a *text*? From Mr. Hart?"

"Yeah."

"How is that even possible?"

"It's another long story. And to tell you the truth I don't know exactly how or why. But don't you think it's weird? That he keeps asking if anything "unusual" has happened? You'd figure he'd be a tad more worried about us. Seeing as how we're kids, and he's supposed to be in charge."

"You are totally not making any sense," Brandon says. "What do you mean he *keeps* asking if anything unusual has happened? Since when?"

"Never mind," I say. "I'll explain later. Right now I need to text him back."

I'll tell you what's strange—we have a new app on our phones. Called iTime. Ever hear of it?

I have. Very recently.

What's it doing on our phones?

It wasn't meant for you.

Then how did it get here?

By accident.

How so?

You tell me. You must have gone to the basement of the general store. It's the only thing that makes sense.

We did.

Did someone fool around with somebody's MacBook?

Maybe.

There you go.

"There you go"? What in the heck is that supposed to mean? We're gathered around my phone now, all of us, and there's really only one thing we care about at this point. So I type it in. *Mr. Hart, do you know where we are?* I would say that's a direct question, wouldn't you? All I'm asking for is a straight answer. Instead, I get this:

I have an idea.

Have you ever heard of something called T.G.W., Inc.

I have now.

Now? You mean now *now? I am the first to mention it?*

The second.

So who was the first then?

It's difficult to say.

"This guy is playing games," Bev says.

"He thinks it's some kind of joke," says Brandon.

"Who are you communicating with?" says Daniel.

"And how are you doing it? Why are you . . . tapping on that box in your hand?" says Elizabeth.

"It's another long story," I say. "And I doubt you'll believe me." Then I type my message back to Mr. Hart.

Whatever. We're going to reset this and come back. See you soon.

Don't yet. You need to wait.

What for?

There's a loose end.

Loose end?

Right.

Mr. Hart, we really need to come back. We can't do anything about a loose end.

"I don't like it," Bev says.

"Me neither," says Brandon.

"He's pushing it," says Bev. "He's really pushing it. Who does he think he is, anyway? He can't control us. Can he?"

We stare at my phone until we get a final message.

Await further instructions. You MUST NOT come back now under any circumstances. This is nonnegotiable. THERE MAY BE NOTHING TO COME BACK TO!

FIFTY-EIGHT

W E OBVIOUSLY NEED TO think things through a little. Have a freewheeling discussion. In, you know—a democratic fashion.

Even take a vote on what we ought to do next.

But before we can do anything, soldiers come by and herd us out. We're to be taken to McKonkey's Ferry with everyone else, they tell us, and from there we're on our own.

At least it will make Daniel and Elizabeth happy—they'll be that much closer to their farm. What they're going to do about their uncle James and the Hessians in the farmhouse is up to them.

They shuffle us outside and put us back up on horses, though there are no blindfolds this time. None of us get our own horse, of course. We ride behind soldiers. I'm with the same guy as last time—he didn't introduce himself then, and doesn't trouble himself to do so now. About twenty yards away is His Excellency, General George Washington, majestic upon his white steed, but he takes no special notice of us.

It is cold, dark for this time of the afternoon, and a few flakes of snow are falling, but everyone knows, in their bones, that this isn't the worst of it, not by a long shot. You don't even need the Weather Channel app to know that something big and bad and nasty is just about to blow. The sky's got that dark, ominous, foreboding thing going on, like it's getting ready to punch you in the mouth.

General Washington says something to General Greene, who relays the message to a burly fellow, who quickly bellows: "Forward ho!" Then our procession, led by His Excellency General Washington, moves out at a fairly quick pace, and we follow, two by two. Five minutes later, we are on little more than a path in the woods. The snow is falling a little more heavily upon us, and beginning to cover our heads and hats and shoulders. Little white patches collect on our horses' long muzzles, and they snort every once in a while to shake it off.

I try to twist around, to see if I can see any of my fellow travelers, but it's tricky, as I don't want to fall off the horse. But I see Brandon in the row behind me. I see Daniel and Elizabeth. Then, just as I'm about to turn around on my horse, I see something else.

I see ol' Butt-Ugly himself, Mr. Kramm, dressed now in Continental regalia, riding Bev's horse. And sitting behind him, Bev.

He sees me seeing him, and the first thing he does is put a finger to his lips.

The second thing he does is jerk his thumb backward, toward Bev.

And the third thing he does is slice his thumb across his own neck. Meaning Bev's neck.

I have a funny feeling that I just found *the loose end* Mr. Hart was talking about.

I turn around, facing front. Or, rather, the back of my rider.

Did I just see what I thought I saw?

I do the math. Daniel and Elizabeth's farmhouse. The stable. Two Hessians, one wounded.

And one missing.

So Kramm must have gotten away and followed us.

I twist around, get a second look.

Kramm pretends not to see me now. He keeps his eyes ahead, his head straight. Behind him, Bev doesn't have clue one about her rider, Mr. Kramm, or the thumb across his throat.

Meanwhile, we've made progress. What was a mere country path, wide enough for two horses, has become something pretty much like a recognizable *road*. And there are more stone farmhouses scattered along the way now, not so very far from each other, as they were before.

And there's also, dotted here and there, red barns, stone millhouses, woodsheds, and broken-down fences. As we pass one homestead we see children, maybe five or six years old, doing chores. Their father wears a wide-brimmed hat—and seems displeased to see our caravan passing by. The children, though, wish us a good Christmas, at least until they are shushed by their dad.

"We won't be long now," says my rider. "We'll be coming into camp. The men are none too happy, if you want to know, laddie. They are hungry and cold and tired and plain wore down. Best not to say a word with any. They might tear your head off."

A few minutes later we come to the edge of the camp. There are a few tents, a few fires for cooking, and huddled everywhere are the men. Some have their muskets with them, but most do not. They're sullen. Dirty. Their clothes are in some cases little more than rags, and a few have nothing at all on their feet. Plus, they smell.

No one stands at attention or in any way officially acknowledges our procession.

No one salutes General Washington, or anyone else.

These are the guys His Excellency is counting on?

On this sorry, ragged group rides the revolution?

Our procession clomps through and then stops. "It's the end of the line for you and your mates," says my rider. "We've brought you as far as we're bringing you. If I was you, I'd run back to me mum and dad. It's Christmas Day still, laddie. You ought to be home, not out here with the likes of us."

"You're probably right," I say. "I'll just get our group together and then off we go. I thank you for the ride."

He tips his hat, and then he's gone.

I turn around: everyone's dismounted. I see Brandon and Daniel and Elizabeth.

And Bev is merely peeved, per usual. But she has not been harmed, or *taken.*

No Kramm. He got to where he wanted to go, which is the camp. He would have no further use of Bev, who would only slow him down at this point.

While I'm wondering how much of the blame is on me—probably all of it—I turn on my phone to see if there are any texts from Mr. Hart. I'm not surprised that there are none.

"Mel," says Bev. "We're not needed anymore. They can do this without us. Let's go home." She takes out her own phone, turns it on. "I'm running low on power," she says. "So we better hurry. What do we have to do to reprogram this iTime app? And get back to where we belong?"

"I'm with Bev," says Brandon. "It's getting too cold to be cool. Besides, I already know how it turns out. We win. They lose." Brandon takes out his iPhone, and awaits instruction.

"Mel," says Bev, "say goodbye to your friends. Tell them they will live long and prosper." She waves goodbye to Daniel and Elizabeth.

"Right now, we're going to have to stay put," I say. "Remember that loose end Mr. Hart mentioned? I think I know what it is."

"Mel," says Bev, "don't be so *dramatic*. Seriously. You want to hang out, go right ahead. Not me. I don't even like to *read* about history, never mind live in it."

"Dudes," says Brandon, "this is starting to get to be not so cool. Mel, what's the deal? Can we go? I've had enough."

"We can't go," I say. "I told you, there's a loose end."

"The loose end is in Mel's head, Brandon," Bev says.

"Mel?" says Brandon.

"There's a Hessian dude. Mr. Kramm, he calls himself. He's here somewhere, in camp. He rode Bev in. And I'm pretty sure that until he kills General Washington, his mission isn't finished."

FIFTY-NINE

"**W**HO'S THIS GUY?" says Brandon.

"A *Hessian* guy. He goes by the name of Kramm. He's wearing a leather satchel that has the letters T.G.W., INC. on it. And did you notice the message when we opened up the iTime app? Something about the aim is to play, to mess about. Brought to you by T.G.W., Inc. Remember?"

"No," says Brandon. "I don't. And what does it mean, anyway? T.G.W, Inc.?"

"I have no idea, but it doesn't matter. Because how could this guy be carrying a bag with the same initials that are appearing on our phone? I'll tell you how. They're *connected*. And another thing: the guy has a German *Luger*. How can you explain that?"

Brandon rolls his eyes. "Okay, dude," he says. "Whatever you say."

"I'm telling you," I persist. "He's dressed as a Continental soldier now. He was riding the horse Bev was on. So in case you're wondering, no, we can't go back, because yes, we're the ones who are going to have to make sure it doesn't happen. If not us, then who?"

"So what are we?" say Brandon. "Like the Secret Service?"

"Pretty much. Call us what you want. But we have to make sure nothing happens to General Washington. Either before the crossing or after."

"All right, I've had it," says Bev. "I'm tired, I'm sore from riding on the back of a horse, and I kind of think I should maybe take a shower—have you noticed that *everyone* kind of stinks around here?" She glances at Daniel and Elizabeth. "Sorry, no offense, but ... well, this whole thing is getting kind of hard to *take*. I don't care about somebody named Kramm. I really don't. I just want to get out of here." Bev checks her phone. "What was that app you were talking about, Mel? iTime? Here it is, on my home screen." She taps it, and the app opens up.

Brandon and Daniel and Elizabeth gather around.

"Look," says Bev. "It has the time, the date, and the coordinates. The date is December 25, 1776. I'm just going to change the year and then hit *Submit,* and that will be the end of that. You boys want to come along?"

"What about the Hessian dude?" Brandon says.

"What about him?"

"Are we just going to leave him?"

"Brandon," Bev says. "Let me explain it to you. Sometimes the only thing anyone can do is just look out for number one. And right now is one of those times. You coming?"

"So the answer is yes. We'd leave the Hessian dude behind."

"They're smart guys, Brandon. They'll figure something out."

"You sure?"

"Brandon—I'm not arguing. I'm leaving. Better some of us get out than none of us." She holds up her phone. "Who's coming with me? Who wants to go home?"

Home, she says.

A funny word. Considering none of us are home, that is. We're at school. Because, for one reason or another, there was no home for any of us this year.

I can't believe they'd do this. It's like they're seceding from the Union.

But both Bev and Brandon reset the iTime app.

"What does this mean?" Elizabeth says.

"It means goodbye," Bev says. "It was nice knowing you. Mel? You coming?"

"Not yet," I say. "Not when there's a loose end."

"Good luck with that," Bev says. She counts down, three, two, one, then she and Brandon raise their fingers. All they have to do is hit *Submit* and it will be done.

SIXTY

BUT THEY DON'T.

Bev and Brandon stand there, iPhones in their left hand, right forefingers in midair, eyes wide as windows.

"I can't believe we're staying," Bev says. "We must be idiots."

"Maybe we're patriots," I say.

Bev rolls her eyes. Then she sighs. Then we start arguing all over again.

Me against Bev.

Bev against Brandon.

Daniel tries to say something, but Elizabeth tells him to shush, so they start arguing too. Why should we have all the fun?

I see what's happening to us.

We're becoming *factionalized*.

Our interests, our goals, and our needs are *mismatched*.

The colony of Bev has nothing in common with the colony of Brandon.

The colony of Brandon is remote, in every way, from the colony of Mel.

Which results in friction. And arguing. Loudly.

All the stuff that has been sort of kept under the lid for the last few days starts to come out—pretty much at the very worst possible time.

Brandon calls Bev a stuck-up snoot. And then he says she's not really smart at all, she just likes to *pretend* she's smart. Like an *actress*.

He must have hit home, because Bev's eyes flare. And then she *snorts*, she's so mad. "Oh yeah?" Bev says. "You're nothing but a dopey loser, Brandon. You don't even belong at the Fredericksville School. You'll never catch up because you're too dumb and too lazy."

"Yeah?" says Brandon. "Well, guess what you are, Bev. You're a big drama queen, just like your mother."

Which Bev does not take lying down. She walks up to Brandon, raises her hand, and is about to slap him right across the face when an officer comes by on horseback.

An officer of the Continental Army. With three other soldiers on horseback close behind.

Which, if you want to know the truth, we've kind of forgotten about. The Continental Army? The crossing of the Delaware? Hey—we're arguing here! First things first!

"Silence!" the officer says, trying to shout over us. "Silence! Or you all will be bound and gagged, I promise!"

That stops us.

"Who are you children, and what business have you here?" he says. He glances down at my feet, and then he notices Brandon's hoodie. He's about to comment when Bev butts in.

"And who are you?" says Bev.

"He is Captain Joseph Moulder, of the Philadelphia Battalion of Associators," says one of the men. "And no more impertinent questions from you, young miss."

"My charge," says Captain Moulder, "is to patrol this perimeter and to maintain order. You will cease making any further commotion, or I shall have you bound and gagged. Now for the last time: state your business."

"Our fathers are soldiers," says Elizabeth. "We came to bring them what little food we had to spare."

It's a good line, and it pretty much works. "Have you done so?" Captain Moulder asks her.

"We have, sir," Elizabeth says.

"Then move along. Go to your homes. Your business at this camp is ended."

SIXTY-ONE

CAPTAIN MOULDER AND HIS Philadelphia Battalion of Associators ride off.

"Well, how do you like that?" I say. "So where were we?"

"We were arguing," says Elizabeth. "Among ourselves."

"Yes, that's right," I say. "And now we need to go warn General Washington. He has to be around here somewhere. Anyone coming with me?"

I start walking.

I know they don't like it, but a minute later all of them start walking along with me.

We come to a dock on the Delaware, where a group of officers are supervising the loading of the men onto a long black boat—the famous longboats used for taking iron ore up and down the river. Each one can hold as many as thirty men. It's nearly five in the evening now, and already dark. The snow is really starting to fall down, and all the soldiers are grim, cold, and noticeably un-enthusiastic. They must have figured out by now that crossing the Delaware is only the half of it. They are not going to a party, or to anyplace warm or cozy.

Elizabeth takes charge. She walks right up to the most important guy she can find, who turns out to be General Greene. "We demand," she says, "to be taken to General Washington immediately! We have urgent business!"

"Business?" says General Greene. "At a time such as this? And I thought we were quit of you children. Were you not instructed to return to your parents?"

"We must speak with General Washington," I say. "All of us. His life may be in danger."

"You're mad. All of you. Now go away."

"We aren't mad," says Brandon.

"And we're not going away," says Elizabeth.

"General Greene," I say, "if it wasn't for me, General Washington might have canceled this crossing. You know it's true."

"What danger?" he says.

"Mortal danger. But we will tell it only to him."

General Greene thinks it over, and then comes to a decision. "Very well," he says. "If you insist. Let us go to General Washington and you shall have an audience. Of one minute. Do not take a second longer, so help you."

We are led, in single file, up a snowy path lined with

soldiers, to McKonkey's Ferry Inn, which is a good-sized brick-faced building. McKonkey, we've been told, is a guy who runs a ferry service from Pennsylvania to New Jersey, and also houses and feeds travelers. Inside the building, which is warmed by a massive fireplace, is General Washington.

Eating dinner, of all things. And seeming quite comfortable with himself as he does so. I can see on his plate something brown, which I think is meat; something brownish, which might be a vegetable; and something white, which could be a potato. He is dining with three other officers, including Captain Hamilton. If I am not mistaken, all of them are discussing, as we approach, the price of land in the Ohio Valley.

The price of land in the Ohio Valley?

At a time like this?

With the revolution itself hanging by a thread?

Then the conversation turns to things more pertinent. "Your Excellency," says General Greene. "I have my report. A tenth of the troops have gotten across the river. No men have been lost, and few have complained. Plus, another matter to discuss. These—these young people . . . desire to speak with you."

General Washington dabs his lips with a handkerchief. He gives the distinct impression that nothing that General Greene has to say is worth disturbing his meal.

"A tenth?" he says. "That is all?"

"A tenth," says General Greene. "The currents are treacherous, Excellency. Our Marbleheader men at the helms of the longboats are the best we have, but they've no interest in tipping over. Colonel Glover commands the entire operation, and no one dares question him. There are also chunks of ice in the river, some large enough to disturb passage. Sir, Colonel Glover says getting the men across is straightforward enough, if slow. The Marbleheaders are most concerned with bringing across the horses and most especially the cannons. They will wait till last, but the weather and ice are getting worse, far worse. And we must get everything across. We cannot attack without a full army. Or without cannon."

"But only a tenth, General Greene? At what time— nearly six? We are far behind schedule, are we not?"

"We are, sir. It is a miserable night for a crossing. The Marbleheaders are doing the best they can, under difficult circumstances."

"I would dine easier, General Greene, if they moved faster. Our attack is planned for before dawn, not after."

"I'm aware, Excellency. Acutely aware. We are moving the men at the fastest pace we can."

"Very well, General. And what else have you brought me? Not these infernal children again. I thought I had seen the last of them. What tall tales do they wish to inflict upon me this time?"

"They wish to warn you, sir."

"They what?"

"They wish to warn you."

"About what?" General Washington says, and turns his big head to me.

"Your Excellency, your life is in danger!" I say.

General Washington responds with a hearty laugh, and as soon as he does the other men at his table join in. The merriment is positively contagious.

"Of course it is," he says. "As are the lives of us all. But I make it a firm policy not to let the threat of my demise come between me and my plum pudding." This provokes another round of hilarity, and someone nearly falls off his chair. The general seems quite pleased with himself. "Now run along. Consider your warning delivered, and thank you very much."

I persist. "But General Washington, I mean specifically, your life is in danger. From the man at the farm. Who burned down the horse stable. He's followed us here."

The general stops eating and glares at me. "I believe I said, and said most clearly, that this matter shall never be talked of again. Did I not?"

I can see I'm not getting anywhere, and I'd rather not be taken out to the firing squad like he promised. So I try one last time to warn him. "It could come from a bullet or a knife. Or even poison in the food you're eating."

The general takes a bite from his plum pudding, and frowns. "My word," he says. "If this be poison, I shall have the whole thing. Most delectable indeed!"

Yet one more round of laugher, merriment, hilarity. One officer nearly chokes on his sherry.

It stinks, sometimes, being a kid. No one takes you seriously.

SIXTY-TWO

THEN, WITHOUT ANY FURTHER ceremony, General Washington returns to dinner. General Greene whispers something in the ear of Captain Hamilton, and the next thing we know, Captain Hamilton himself is escorting us out of McKonkey's inn.

"Whatever you say with respect to his personal safety, he will hear none of it," says Captain Hamilton. "We have tried in the past. He is utterly impervious to our entreaties. He does not think himself invincible, merely destined. And no bullet or blade yet made could ever mar his destiny. Or so he believes. He will not heed any warning you bring, or any that we bring."

"I'm not making this up, Captain Hamilton," I say. "You saw him for yourself—the man at the horse stable.

A Hessian by the name of Kramm. He's followed us. He's in this camp right now. And he's going to try to kill General Washington whether the general believes it or not. Can you assign him bodyguards?"

"We did have personal guards for him, but those men have been deployed elsewhere. There did not seem to be any danger on this side of the Delaware."

"Then we shall do it," says Elizabeth. "We shall stay close to his person, and protect him. We have not been assigned elsewhere, so therefore he cannot object."

"But only soldiers are allowed close to him," says Captain Hamilton.

"Then we shall enlist."

"You cannot. At this hour? And you, if I may point out, are not—you are not . . ."

"A gentleman?"

Captain Hamilton blushes. "Of age," he says.

"A pair of breeches takes care of the first part," Elizabeth says. "As for the second, I have seen lads our age in your army. As for the last part, simply assign us to a battalion, Captain Hamilton. You need not do more. No one will ask to see our papers, or question our authenticity. And we shall take care of the rest."

"You remind me of myself," Captain Hamilton says. "How old are you?"

"Twelve," I say.

"All of you?"

"Yes."

"When I was twelve I was working in a counting house. On an island in the Caribbean Sea of which I suspect you have never heard. My mother had died and my father was long gone. And I remember I told myself: all I need is the one chance. If providence shall but provide me the one chance, I swear upon all that is holy that I shall do the rest. My chance, it did come, and I do say I have made the most of it. So I shall give you your chance. I believe the Massachusetts Twenty-Third Continental Regiment could use extra men. I will pass word to its commander, Colonel Bailey. From there it will be up to you to convince him that you are indeed men—not boys and girls.

"Remember this: once on the other side, should you get detached from your unit, and should you happen upon a person whom you know not to be friend or foe, we have developed a code. The call is 'Victory.' The response is 'Or death.' Should you call 'Victory' and not hear 'Or death' in response, you shall know you have an enemy upon you. If you have a weapon, charge forward. If you have no weapon, fall back. But prudently. Let it not be said of any soldier in the Continental Army that he lost his wits and fled in panic. The worst is not death. The worst is eternal ignominy.

"Wait here," he says. "Outside. Your orders and detachment duty will be by presently." Captain Hamilton turns, and goes back to McKonkey's Ferry Inn to finish his dinner.

"What are we going to do?" Brandon says. "Make like we've enlisted?"

"That's the plan," I say. "And it's the only one we've got."

SIXTY-THREE

THE SNOW AND SLEET and freezing rain fall heavier still, and the wind starts whipping around. It's brutal. Standing around waiting makes it worse. We'll get hypothermia if we don't do something.

We set about transforming Elizabeth and Bev from girls to boys, but we don't have any luck. Daniel looks for an extra pair of breeches in somebody's tent, but every piece of good clothing is already taken. Elizabeth and Bev duck inside the tent anyway, and do what they can to pass themselves off as boys. It's not much, but it will have to do. And Bev says there's no way she's going to lose either her jacket or her earmuffs.

So that leaves Brandon and me. I kind of fit in except for my white Nikes. Brandon? He still has on jeans, sneakers, and his red hat with the lobo on it, which doesn't fit in at all. But we have to go with what we've got.

A boy not much older than us comes along and tells us to follow him. "Your orders are in," he says. "I've been told to come and fetch you."

This doesn't work for me—my plan was to stay as close as possible to wherever General Washington happens to be. "We can't leave," I say. "We're needed right here."

"Have you taken the oath?"

"Of course we have," I lie.

"Then you'll come with me. To the Twenty-Third Continental Regiment. And there's no sense in arguing. Believe me, I've tried. No one cares to listen."

The boy nods, insisting that we follow him.

"Come," says the boy. "Or I shall be obliged to report you for dereliction of duty."

"I think we better go," says Elizabeth.

I don't really agree, but I'm kind of shuffled along. The boy leads us to where the troops of the Massachusetts Twenty-Third Continental are gathered, far back in the line of men waiting to cross the river. There are maybe seventy or eighty men in the unit. Every single one of them is cold, miserable, and scrawny. Finally the boy passes us to Colonel Bailey, a lanky guy with a rough beard and torn blue coat.

"Wait here until further notice," Colonel Bailey tells us. "Maintain silence. And try your best not to do anything stupid.

"And you," he says to Bev. "What be your name?"

"Stevens," she says.

"Your Christian name?"

"E-Edward." Bev kind of squares her shoulders and looks the guy in the eye. We're lucky it's pretty dark by now.

"Edward?"

"Edward."

"You be sure?"

"I be sure."

"And you?" he says to Elizabeth. "Your name?"

"Michael," Elizabeth says. "Michael ... um ... Michael Brown."

It doesn't seem like Colonel Bailey is buying it, but probably he has more important things to think about just now. He addresses himself to the whole unit. "Men," he says, "and others: we will wait until so ordered to board one of the longboats you see below at the dock. It seems to be a rather lengthy process, due to the snow and the ice forming in the river. When our turn comes we will be commanded by Colonel Glover, and by the Marblehead men. We will do as they tell us, and we will make quick work of it. Remember to keep your muskets and powder as dry as you can—your lives, and our cause, depend upon it. Maintain silence. We know not where the enemy hides his ears."

There are grunts from our comrades. And then Brandon gives me a nudge.

"Mel. I've been thinking."

"Glad to hear that, Brandon."

"I'm thinking it maybe doesn't make a whole lot of sense to be standing around here. We've kind of deactivated ourselves."

"That's what I was worried about in the first place. We should have stayed at McKonkey's Ferry Inn. As close to Washington as possible."

"Maybe you were right."

"Maybe I was. Kramm could be anywhere, waiting for his opportunity.

"There are hundreds of guys standing around, and it's pretty much dark. We can't just stand here, Brandon. We're going to have to do something."

"Concur," Brandon says. "And if we find him? Any idea what we should do with him?"

"We turn him in to General Washington. And General Washington's rope. The one he uses for spies."

SIXTY-FOUR

"**B**OYS," SAYS BEV. "What are we whispering about?"

"It's not a good use of our resources," I say, "for all five of us to be standing around here doing nothing."

"We're not doing nothing," says Daniel. "We're in line. To board a longboat, which will take us across the river."

"But the point is not to get across the river," I say. "The point is to make sure that nothing happens to General Washington *before* he crosses the river."

"What exactly," says Elizabeth, "do you propose?"

"I propose that you and Bev stay right here. Hold our spots. Daniel, Brandon, and I are going to search around for Kramm, and we'll report back in ten minutes."

"No way," says Bev. "The boys get to go, and the girls get to stay? Since when were you put in charge, Mel?"

"Do you want to stand around and argue again, Bev? Or do you want to do something?"

"I'll stay," Daniel says. "Will that solve it? Elizabeth and I. You three go. We'll keep your spots."

Elizabeth glares at her brother, but the deal is struck. Brandon slips off to the right and Bev to the left. I take the center path. It's not hard. It's dark, and snowing, and there are already lots of people milling about and walking around.

Way too many people, as a matter of fact.

I don't even know who's a soldier, who's an officer, and who's just a faker, like me.

It's getting darker and still darker. And the snow is falling harder and harder. Everybody keeps their heads down to protect themselves from the wind and snow. And, to make it even harder, I don't have a flashlight, a candle, a match, or a torch. I have nothing to see by, and I don't dare use my iPhone's flashlight app—every soldier around would immediately jump out of their boots if they saw such a thing. Assuming they had boots, that is.

So I'm not able to identify anyone unless I grab him by the shoulder and get nose to nose. Which is what I start doing. I find a bunch of New Hampshire men and try to check them one by one. It takes a few minutes, and no one's particularly cooperative with a kid like me, but I get through them well enough. No Kramm among them.

Next group I come to is feisty and loud. I ask who they are, and a soldier says they're the First Regiment,

MacDougall's New York Continentals. They've ignored the word to keep the noise down. They think it's more amusing to make loud and vulgar comments about the ongoing scene. What's gotten their attention is the spectacle of a bunch of landlubbing Vermonters venturing onto one of the longboats.

"That soldier, he's like a cat on a kettle," says one. "I'd bet a pretty penny he falls into the drink before the night is done."

"I'd bet a pretty penny you don't have a pretty penny to your name," says another. "And if you did, I'd pry it from you. You still owe me from last month, if memory serves."

"I'll throw you both headfirst into the drink if you don't pipe it down," says a third. "Haven't you got it through your thick skulls? We've been told to be silent. On account of spies lurking here, there, and everywhere."

I walk among the New Yorkers, checking every face I can. No Kramm. Just as I'm about to leave them and examine the men from Maryland, one of the New Yorkers grabs me by the arm.

"And what 'ave we 'ere?" he says. "What you be up to, lad?" The guy, who is maybe a half-inch taller than me, is also smelly, stinky, and foul, in that order.

On his feet are rags, wrapped twice around. His bare toes stick out. His toes are black, which I hope is only filth.

"Are you thievin'?" he says. "You can't wait, until we die a decent death?"

"I'm not a thief," I say.

"Then what are you, poking about like this? A spy?"

We've now gathered some attention among the New York men. They have nothing to do besides stand around and wait to board one of the longboats, which doesn't appear likely to happen anytime soon, so pestering some strange interloper—that would be me—must seem like a pleasant diversion.

"A spy?" says another. He's taller than the first, but just as smelly. He has on his feet something resembling shoes, but not by a whole lot. "Show me a spy and I'll rip his heart out, along with his liver. It'd make a tasty meal, and more than I've had in days. Where be your spy, mate?"

"Right 'ere 'e is," says Shorty. "Spyin' about, looking us all up, one by one. Spyin' or thieving, one or the other. How's about we share his heart, mate? I'll rip out the left side and you can have the right." Then Shorty pokes me in the chest—right where my heart is—and draws a line up and down. "Or would you prefer, my Lord, tops to bottoms?"

"Why, Your Majesty," says the tall one. "I shall take the top of the heart, leave you the bottom. Has anyone salt for the tasting? The last heart I et was a wee bit on the chewy side, don't you know."

The men laugh, kick me in the butt, and send me on my way. New Yorkers—what jokers, whatever the century.

I search around with no success until I hear Brandon loudly—*very* loudly—whispering.

"Mel! Over here! Down by the water!"

I scramble through the crowd of Marylanders and a crowd of Massachusetts men. Brandon is down by the river, next to the loading dock. Only two longboats can be loaded at a time, one on either side of the dock. The Vermonters are still being brought aboard, and the Marblehead men, who both command the loading operation and pilot the longboats, are hissing in an enraged whisper at nearly everyone to shut up and sit down.

"I've seen him, I think," Brandon says. "The Hessian dude. He's in the middle of that boat right there."

Brandon points. A longboat, black, big, bulky, and slow, is making its way across the river. Fore and aft in the boats are Marblehead men, one the oarsman and the other the pilot. Everyone else is sitting down.

"Are you sure you saw him?" I ask Brandon. "It's dark."

"I'm sure. He was the guy at the farmhouse with the torch, right? Short and ugly? But I'm pretty sure he saw me. What I don't understand is why he would go across the river. Washington's on this side. How's he going to get to Washington from over there?"

I think it through. And it makes perfect sense. On this side of the Delaware there are hundreds of men clumped together, and wherever Washington goes he is surrounded. But once Washington crosses over and begins the march to Trenton, his protection will break down. We'll be marching along a road that is unfamiliar. At some point the general could be completely exposed. And totally vulnerable.

"He's going to take up a position, Brandon," I say. "Somewhere along the route he'll find the perfect place. For the kill shot."

SIXTY-FIVE

"**M**EL?" SAYS BRANDON.

"Yeah?"

"What do we do now?

"I'm not sure. I think we've got to think of something. Like, pretty quick."

"Boys?" says a voice behind us. "Are we whispering again?"

It's Bev, who seems very pleased with herself. "So it turns out," she says, "that it's pretty easy to pass as a boy. All you have to do is walk around like you know where you're going. And spit once in a while."

I point to the longboat crossing the river. "The dude we're after is on that one, Bev. Brandon spotted him. Any ideas?"

"So he's going to the other side of the river?"

"Yep."

"Why?"

"I guess he figures his chances are better there, so he can have a shot at Washington without so many people around."

Bev takes this in. A new group of men begin boarding an empty longboat that just came into the dock. "Why don't we just get in line with these guys," she says, "and take this one over?"

It's as good a plan as any. We mix in with the men, and a few minutes later everyone in front of us has boarded and it's our turn.

Or it should be our turn.

Blocking our way is one of the Marbleheaders, the tough fishermen from Marblehead, Massachusetts, who've been given command of the longboats. Their job is to board the men on the longboats one by one and situate them according to some seaman's algorithm, the purpose being, I take it, not to have too many men cram up in the front, or in the back, or on one side or the other, and tip the thing over right there in front of everyone. So he has power, this guy. He has red cheeks and black eyes. "Just where," he says, "do you think you're going?"

"We're with them," I say.

"With who?"

"Them," I say, pointing to the men on the longboat.

The Marbleheader rolls his eyes. "Not likely. Now run

along. This boat be full and ready to shove off." Then the guy puts his hand to my chest and shoves *me* off.

I stumble backward. Unfortunately for me, I lose my footing, stumble off the dock, and fall on my butt. Right in the middle of the muddy pathway the men have been using to come to the dock itself.

And even more unfortunately, I have an audience.

Quite a large audience, if you want to know the truth.

The men from Pennsylvania, New York, and Maine, to be exact.

Who see me sitting on my butt and laugh in unison.

Laughing, unlike mere smiling, is generally a noise-producing event. Har-har, ho-ho, hee-hee—you get the idea.

A hundred men of the soldiering kind laughing in unison—that's definitely a noise-producing event.

So much so that the Marbleheader who shoved me hisses at the men to quiet down.

So much so that the noise draws the attention of some officers, who immediately come down to the dock and also hiss at the men to quiet down. Some rather rude and vulgar language is exchanged by both sides. The officers are adamant that the men comport themselves in a certain manner, and the men, who have been standing around in the snow and driving sleet for hours now and are about to board boats to take them into battle, are not in the mood to be told what to do and what not to do.

Things get a little tense.

The officers are hardly older than the men. It's a mystery to me how the few get to be officers and the many get to be mere men, but it is what it is. Bev and Brandon help me to my feet. "That wasn't cool, dude," Brandon says to the Marbleheader, who merely shrugs. Bev is about to go off on the guy, but I tell her to take it easy.

"We're still going to need him," I say.

"He's a total jerk," Bev says. "He didn't have to push you."

"Maybe not, but we still haven't solved our problem. We are on this side, and Kramm is on the other."

We turn and watch as the boatmen shove off and the longboat begins crossing. There are chunks of ice floating by, and it's snowing and sleeting and awful, but we're able to make progress.

About thirty men are aboard. The sides of the boat are high, and the pilot and the captain are standing, so we can see their heads. The longboat takes a distinct northward tack to counter the current, which will push it downstream, to reach the landing zone on the Jersey side. There's one guy at the helm of the boat, using a long pole to push away ice, and there's a guy in the stern, with his hand upon another long pole, a steering sweep, which is affixed to the deck. There's also one guy on each side manning an oar, and they work in tandem. All the boatman are Marbleheaders, and they know what they're doing. Everyone else is a landlubber, and just along for the ride.

The boat starts to inch its way upstream.

This is going to take a *very* long time.

"We really need to get across," says Bev.

"Yeah, but I don't think they're going to let us on until our unit goes," I say. "That seems to be how they're doing it. And I don't think our unit is set to go. They're still up on the hill. Maybe we should go back and wait with Daniel and Elizabeth."

"That's not going to cut it," says Bev. "You know that, right, Mel?"

I know it all right. I just don't know what to do about it.

SIXTY-SIX

S OMETIMES YOU DON'T HAVE a single good idea to
your name. And the harder you try to come up with
one, the harder it gets.

And sometimes while you're trying to think of a good
idea, but can't, what you need kind of walks up to you and
bops you on the head.

Which is how things happen next. General Washington, General Greene, and Captain Hamilton come down
the dock to see for themselves what the commotion is all
about.

And to inform Colonel John Glover that the general
is ready to cross.

The snow is getting worse. It's driving now, pelting all
of us, starting to blow full force. I think the commander
in chief wants to get across before it's too late.

General Greene has a word with Colonel Glover, and space in the next boat is cleared. I catch Captain Hamilton's eye, and he nods me over. "You have something," he says, "on your mind?"

"I do," I say. "We have to get on the next boat. It's urgent."

"Urgent why?"

"We saw our Hessian friend. He's already crossed. He's waiting on the other side."

"Are you certain?"

"One hundred percent."

"The general will not countenance any delay. Nothing must interfere."

"Everything's at risk, whether it's part of the plan or not. If you just let us get on the next boat, we'll be able to protect him, but he'll never have to know. So he won't say no."

"How many are you?"

Me, and Bev, and Brandon, and Daniel, and Elizabeth: five, I tell him.

"Impossible. Three of you at most."

I know it's the best deal I'm going to get, so there's nothing to do except agree. I tell Captain Hamilton we're good. He tells me to line up right behind him, and he'll see to it we get aboard.

That leaves only one task.

"I'll be right back," I say to Brandon. "Hold my place." I turn and run before either he or Bev asks me to explain myself.

The Massachusetts Twenty-Third Continental Regiment is maybe seventy or eighty yards away. The snow is really starting to fall now, and as I run down the line I go past all the different militias and companies lining up to board the longboats. In the dark and snow I can't identify where they're from, or see their colors, if they have any. They could be from Connecticut or Delaware or New Jersey or New York or Maryland or Virginia, but every man is in exactly the same condition—cold and wet. I keep going till I get to Daniel and Elizabeth, at the very back of the pack of the Twenty-Third Continental.

Getting here is the easy part. Now I have to tell Daniel and Elizabeth we're going over now, and they're going over later. It doesn't help that I have about six seconds to do it. Or that we're standing next to a riverbank, surrounded by two thousand soldiers, in a driving snowstorm. I'm not going to have time to soothe anyone's feelings, soften the blow, talk it out—or listen to counterarguments.

Or indulge a hissy fit.

This is war.

Orders must be given, and taken.

"Mel!" says Daniel, as I approach. "We were getting concerned. Your friends—have they met with misfortune?

"They're fine," I say. "But here's the deal. We spotted Kramm, and we can't let him get too far ahead of us. Captain Hamilton will only allow three to ride over on the next boat. I'm thinking it's best if Brandon, Bev, and I stick together—I don't think we can risk being separated. Okay? I think you two should stay with the Twenty-Third and get over as fast as you can. Remember the call, guys. It's 'Victory.' And the response is—"

"Or death," say Daniel and Elizabeth in unison.

"And we'll have to catch up somehow on the other side," I say. "We can't worry about how. We'll have to figure it out once we all get over. Agreed?"

"Agreed," says Daniel.

Elizabeth offers her hand. "Be careful," she says, and I tell her I will.

Then I'm off, and I get in line behind Captain Hamilton with a second to spare.

SIXTY-SEVEN

MAYBE IT WOULD BE more impressive if the sun were shining, trumpets were blaring, and General Washington, like a pharaoh in ancient Egypt, was brought down to the dock in a golden chariot.

But that's not how it happens. Through the driving storm, with big, flat chunks of ice clogging up the Delaware, General George Washington stands at the top of the dock, looks across the river to New Jersey, then walks down the dock, and waits.

No speech.

No trumpets, and no rockets' red glare.

The general has a word with Colonel Glover, and then the boarding begins. Captain Hamilton goes first. Following him are a couple of officers, and then, without ceremony, General George Washington, all six feet two inches of him, walks aboard. Colonel Glover has hold of his left arm, and, as General Washington steps aboard, Captain Hamilton takes him by his right arm.

The Father of Our Country is grim, but very determined. But I'm not sure he's entirely in his comfort zone sitting on a boat. I'd bet anything he'd rather be sitting on his horse.

Eight men follow. I'm counting, because I'm worried that at the last second they'll run out of room.

But they don't. Bev and Brandon and I are last in line, and Colonel Glover waves us on. I think General Washington notices—he shakes his head just a bit, and looks even grimmer, if that's possible—but doesn't give the order to toss us out.

Every set of eyes on the Pennsylvania side watches.

Then we're off.

That is to say, we're pushed away from the dock, and we begin our journey across the Delaware River.

Five feet out, the weather gets worse. Or maybe it was this bad in the first place, but we didn't know it on land.

Wind. Freezing snow pelting our faces. Totally, one hundred percent awful.

Now we're maybe seven feet out. Nobody on the dock appears much farther away, that's for sure. And the other side? The bank on the New Jersey side, where we're headed? Might as well be a million miles away.

The Marbleheaders manning our boat start cursing

under their breaths. The chunks of ice clogging up the river bang against our boat, making horrible scraping noises. One particularly large chunk, maybe about the size of a big hot tub, slams into us.

First we rock, then we roll. And I think: *Did that put a hole in the hull? How sturdy is this thing, anyway?*

"Think we're going to sink?" Brandon says. His red hat is white with snow and slush.

"Nah," I say. "They know what they're doing."

"I hope you're right," Bev says. Her eyes are wide, and her face is white, but there's no tremble in her voice. It must be her acting gene.

"Bev?" I say. "You okay?"

She nods as though saying yes, but her eyes say no.

"It's going to be fine," I tell her. Not that it's so great right now. We're what—twenty feet from where we started?

Thirty?

I don't know why it's taking so long. Plus, if you ask me, we're sort of headed wrong. We're headed upstream, against the current, against all the ice flowing downstream. Some of the chunks are poked away by one of the Marbleheaders.

But we are definitely fighting a losing battle. I know the idea was to get to the midpoint of the river, and then we'd go downstream, which is supposed to put us at the designated landing spot on the Jersey side, but this is ridiculous.

We're going backward, not forward, and if I'm not

mistaken, we might be getting closer to the Pennsylvania side, not the New Jersey side.

The Marbleheaders curse.

Someone raises a voice.

From on shore we hear a horse neigh.

Then somebody does something pretty dumb.

If you guess Brandon, you guess right.

"I'm moving up," he says. "I don't like being on the end." He then flashes his iPhone. "I'll get some clips while I'm at it."

"Brandon, this is a small boat," I say. "You can't just move around." Then I try to hold on to him, but it's too late.

Brandon might like to play the dumb one for laughs, and he might not be as dumb as he acts, but sometimes? He can be *totally* dumb. First of all, you don't move around in a small boat crowded with men. There's equilibrium, and balance, and too much weight on one side of the equation and not enough on the other. Second, you don't move around while trying to get across an ice-choked river in a storm.

"Yo, Brandon," I say. "Do you really need to get in the middle of the boat that bad? At the risk of tipping the whole thing over?"

Does Brandon listen to me?

He does not.

Brandon shuffles along the inside edge of the boat. Someone grumbles. Someone curses. We dip, I swear, ten degrees leeward, or maybe it's windward.

The left side goes down and the right side goes up.

Then we get double tapped. First one ice block, then another. We lurch. People bump into each other.

Brandon is shoved, and not too kindly, to the back of the boat, where he belongs.

And in the middle of all this, seven, ten feet away from me, is General George Washington. Our commander in chief. And I have to tell you, he's not like he is in the famous painting of this event, which was painted I don't know how many years after the fact.

First off, our commander in chief isn't that old. He's in his forties, remember. Not like the gray-haired dude in the painting. Second, he doesn't look so terrifically determined and noble to me. I think he's as wet, cold, stressed, worried, and miserable as the rest of us, but he's not about to let any of his men know that. He just stares straight ahead, and *endures.*

Plus, he's nowhere near the front of the boat. He's in the middle, surrounded, and protected, by his men. Who are even colder, wetter, more miserable, and more stressed and worried and afraid than General Washington, because they've got their own lives *and* his life on their minds.

So the truth is? It's just one big ol' misery party. Which doesn't seem like it's ever going to end. But something's happened, kind of while we weren't paying attention. The Marbleheaders have gotten us to the midway point, and now all of a sudden they've turned us and we're heading downstream. And we pick up speed.

We can see the guys on the other side, flickering through the lanterns they've brought. Officers are trying to keep the men in orderly groups and have them move away from the landing area.

We're fifty yards from shore, and we know we're going to do this. Then we're forty yards away, thirty yards, coming up fast.

We're still supposed to keep the noise down here, remember. This is a secret mission, and the idea is to launch a surprise attack.

Brandon, of course, forgets all that. Brandon shouts, loud enough so everyone from here to Trenton can hear: "Yo, everybody! We're gonna make it!"

General George Washington half rises from his seat, sees who is making the commotion, and calls out in a clear, sharp voice: "Silence! Silence, or I shall have your head!"

VICTORY OR DEATH

SIXTY-EIGHT

Gᴇɴᴇʀᴀʟ Wᴀsʜɪɴɢᴛᴏɴ sᴛᴀʀᴇs ʀɪɢʜᴛ at Brandon, who tries to shrink behind three guys in front of him. If Brandon were smart, he'd toss his red hat overboard, or at least put it in his pocket, because the commander-in-chief has no trouble picking him out in a crowd.

"If I hear one more word from that one," General Washington says, "I will be most displeased." Then he turns his great head forward, to the upcoming riverbank.

"Sor-reee," Brandon says in as low a voice as he can manage. "I just got a little excited."

"Zip it, Brandon," Bev says. "Okay?"

Brandon just nods his head, and then we're over on the other side. The New Jersey side.

It's kind of too cold for anyone to jump up and down with joy about it.

First off the boat, naturally, are the men in the front. Captain Hamilton first, then General Greene, then General Washington, and then the rest of us. There's no ceremony. It's the middle of the night now, and only three-quarters of the army is across the river. And Trenton is still nine miles away. Crossing the river isn't getting easier, not in this weather. Add it up, and it hardly seems possible that a predawn strike is possible. We're close enough to General Washington to hear him voicing his concerns, but there's no turning back now—not for General Washington, not for the Continental Army, and not for us, either.

"Let's go, guys," I say. "Kramm's ahead of us somewhere."

"Where did he go?" Bev asks.

"I bet over there," Brandon points. "To those buildings. It's where I'd go, if I wanted to get away from everyone."

General Washington starts conferring with the men who've already landed. The last thing on his mind is us, so we slip away and run up a slope where we can get a view. One of the buildings is a stable. We hear yelling, and then we see Mr. Kramm, on horseback, kick some guy in the face and ride off.

Two minutes later we're in the stables ourselves. The guy who got kicked has picked himself up and is in no mood to negotiate.

"We need horses," I tell him. "That man who kicked you? He's dangerous. He has to be stopped. And we're with the Continental Army."

"The Continental Army?" the guy says. He's an older guy, and he's bigger than us, and angry. "You want anything from me, you'll have to pay in pound sterling. I'll not take worthless Continental scrip, I swear. If you want anything at all at this time of night, and on this day—it's still Christmas, blast it—you'll have to pay double. To make up for that one." He points, with his thumb, toward Kramm, who's now gotten a good head start on us.

But like I said, we don't have a lot of time here. Nor do we have anything like pounds sterling upon our person.

"You're not going to like it," I tell the guy. "But we're taking horses, and we're taking them now. And the Continental Army thanks you."

The guy snarls and cusses and then takes a run at us.

Brandon sticks his foot out and the dude falls flat on his face, which buys us about thirty seconds.

I know it's not nice, but the thing is? We don't have time for nice anymore.

There are only two horses left in the stable, and Brandon starts saddling up one of them—something he learned how to do on his family's ranch in New Mexico. Bev and I keep watch on the stable owner, who's taking his time picking himself up from the snow. Maybe he's starting to realize that there's no use trying to stop us, not with the whole Continental Army coming his way.

"Two is better than one, Brandon," I say. "You ride alone. We'll take the other."

"Can't all three of us fit on one horse?" says Bev.

"We could, but it's not a great idea," I say. "We might have to separate. This way we double our chances."

"You bring these horses back, you hear?" the old man says. "Otherwise it's plain stealing."

"We will," Brandon tells him. "Soon as we're done with them. Promise."

The old man grunts an acceptance of sorts, then stands by as Brandon helps Bev and me get horse number two saddled up. Which is a good thing, since I don't have a clue how to do it.

I put my left foot in the stirrup and hoist myself up. I kind of surprise myself by not immediately falling off. Then Bev gets herself behind me, and we're ready to ride.

The wind's really ripping now. Trees are swaying and creaking like they have a notion to crack and fall over. Now that we're mounted, I glance back at the river. Under the lanterns, in a kind of spooky dull glow, Marblehead men are standing on the docks, and the longboats are returning to pick up more loads. It would be great to see Daniel and Elizabeth coming along, but I guess they're still waiting in the boarding line. To the left of the dock, about fifty yards away, the men have built a bonfire to keep everyone warm, and those that have crossed are standing near it, or feeding it with any wood they can find. I think I spot, in the middle of the men, General Washington. He's a head taller than anyone else.

"Which way?" Brandon yells over the wind.

"We can't tell from here where he went," I holler. "The

Bear Tavern Road is up ahead. It goes for about two miles and then splits off into River Road and Pennington Road. We've got to get to Kramm before he gets to the split. All right?"

"Dude!" shouts Brandon. "How do you know so much?"

"I was paying attention at the reenactment. They explained the whole thing. Don't you remember? Or weren't you paying attention?"

"Neither," Brandon says. "Or is it both?"

"Whatever," I say. "We have to hunt him down. We can't let Kramm get in a shooting position."

Brandon slaps his horse, I slap ours, and we're off.

SIXTY-NINE

BRANDON'S HORSE CHARGES OUT of the gate like it's in a wintertime Kentucky Derby.

Ours?

Not so much.

Bev—remember, she's supposed to be the smart one—takes about a nanosecond to figure out why. She's right behind me. She's holding on to my coat. I hear her yell in my ear: "Mel, have you ever ridden a horse before?"

"Of course," I say. "Plenty of times." It's really, like, never, but how hard can it be?

"You're holding the reins wrong," she says. "The horse doesn't know what you want it to do."

"What makes you such an expert?"

"Riding lessons. If you don't know what you're doing, why did you get in front?"

"All right!" I say. "Okay!" Though it kills me to have to say it, this is, like, absolutely *the* worst time to try to fake my way through. "You want to drive?"

She does.

We have to stop and switch places. She's where she's supposed to be and I'm in the back. Then she grabs the reins, digs her knees into the horse's flanks, and says: "Let's go!"

She's talking to the horse, not to me, and somehow the horse understands that Bev means business.

We take off, like the horse wants to get to Pennington Road more than we do. It's not easy going—snow, sleet, etc.—and the ground is hard, but our mare is now on a mission, so we cover ground faster than a go-cart.

But going fast is only part of the problem. The other part is knowing where to go.

"I think it's up here!" Bev shouts. I really have to hold on now, and we're not only going fast, but also riding rough over the road.

"What's up here?" I shout back.

"Bear Tavern Road!" Bev shouts, and yanks the rein on the right. Our mare makes a hard right turn. I mean hard right. So hard, I nearly fall off. I have to grab Bev's coat to hold on, and practically take her down with me.

We manage to hold on, and our mare makes the right. We can kind of see the outlines of a road of sorts—there's nothing straight ahead of us, but there's trees and bushes on either side—so by the process of deduction we can assume that we're on Bear Tavern Road so long as there is nothing immediately in front of us. I think, *It sure would be good to have a powerful flashlight with us. We'd be able to make out tracks if Kramm had come down this way.*

I twist to turn around. I see the tracks we're making, but it's too dark to see anyone else's.

"Let's go, girl!" Bev shouts. "Give us all you've got!"

She does, and we gain still more speed. And for at least five minutes we fly down Bear Tavern Road. At this speed we'll either overtake Kramm or ride right into Trenton ourselves.

But there's the split to worry about, where the road branches off to Pennington Road and River Road. What if we come to the split and haven't found Kramm? Do we go to the left or the right?

"Where's Brandon?" I yell to Bev. "He's supposed to be in front of us!"

"No clue," Bev yells back. "He must have gotten lost." Then she sees something. "Light!" she shouts. "A house! Fifty yards ahead!"

Wind and freezing rain temporarily obscure our view as a strong hurricane-force gale nearly blows us into the next county. Our mare slips in the snow but regains her footing and we press on. Then we come to a small wood-frame house. The place is lit up by a lantern. In front of the house is a man dressed in nightclothes, and he's wielding a four-foot-long fire iron.

"Who be you?" the man shouts. "State your side so I know where you stand, and be prepared for what will come your way! Are you for the king or are you for the revolution? Answer me, you blasted kids!"

"The revolution," I say, and if the guy throws the fire iron at us I'm going to be really, really teed off.

But he doesn't.

"I shall let you live, then!" the man shouts. "A man just came by—a German—he woke me from a sound slumber. He said to alert my neighbors and to stand fast—the traitors were on the march! 'Traitors,' says I, 'what traitors be these?' 'Washington and his men,' the German says. 'Prepare yourself! Act now and we can stop them!' That's when I got my fire iron and chased him away! The man has his facts wrong! King George can burn for eternity! His soldiers have pillaged our farms and possessions! I told this German man, 'Sir, I am an American now! A newborn patriot! Your information is incorrect! Whoever told you I am a Loyalist is quite mistaken, and I shall be glad to shove this iron in your eye to prove it! If the Continental Army be coming down this way, by God I shall join them myself!'"

"Where did the German guy go?" I say. "Is he here?"

"He continued on his road!" the man shouts. "I know what he's about—he's some blasted Hessian for hire! I should have gutted him when I had the chance!" Then he thrusts the fire iron forward, to show us exactly what he would have done.

SEVENTY

I T IS NOW PITCH-BLACK, and the weather is getting truly awful. Kramm, according to this man, got back on his horse and continued on down Bear Tavern Road. Which appears very dark and bleak to me. And dangerous. This man's house, on the other hand, lit by a single lantern, seems like the most luxurious place in the world.

His name, he tells us, is Thompson. He is a farmer, and at one time he had a wife and six children, but his wife died, four of his children died, and his two remaining daughters live with their husbands in nearby Pennington. He is sixty-three, he tells us, and has lived in this house on Bear Tavern Road for thirty-seven years. And if he had any coffee or tea, he would surely offer it to us.

He says, "If the German be the man you're after, then head straight down. You should find him soon enough.

Bring him to me. I'll fix him once and for all, the blasted Hessian."

"I guess we should go," I say to Bev. I have to shout, as the wind has picked up yet again.

"Go where?"

I point. "Down Bear Tavern Road."

"We'll never find him," Bev says. "He could be anywhere."

"Can't we follow his tracks?"

"We can't see anything," Bev says. "Fifty yards from here and it will be pitch-black. And in this weather, it would be dangerous. If we fall, it could be the end of us."

"We can't just do nothing," I say. "We have to do *something*, don't we?" And I think to myself, *Even if it's stupid, completely and utterly stupid, it's better to do* something *rather than* nothing, *right?*

"We might need help," Bev says.

"We don't have any," I say.

"I think we might," she says. "I hear someone coming."

Sure enough, I hear a horse's hooves pounding down the road. Then familiar voices. First Daniel's. Then Elizabeth's.

Then: "Dudes! That you?"

It's Brandon, of course, and he brought company: Daniel and Elizabeth, who somehow bumped their way to the front of the boat-boarding line. All three of them are atop a very small horse, who doesn't seem pleased with the load. "Dudes," Brandon says. "Where were you?"

"We were here," I say. "Did you get lost?"

"I must have. So I went back, and there was Daniel and Elizabeth. But the big news is, everyone's over now, even the horses and the cannons! They're right behind us!"

Bev turns our horse so we can see. Then Daniel calls out: "They're coming! Down the road! The Continental Army! What a sight to behold!"

It is a sight indeed.

In the dead of night, in the depth of winter, in the blackest hour, in the bleakest moment, in the most hopeless circumstances, here they come: the Continental Army of the United States of America.

They are marching, all 2,400 of them, in a column five men across. The storm is in full blow, letting loose a wintry mixture of wind, snow, and sleet, and most of the troops are thoroughly soaked, but it—the storm—doesn't really matter anymore. They've gotten across the Delaware, and are on the march to Trenton: nothing on this man's earth can stop them now.

The soldiers in the first row see the five of us on the front porch, and one man calls out, "Victory!"

"Or death!" we call back in unison.

"Be you soldiers," says the man, "then fall in. And watch as we put the fear of a free people into King George's hired Hessians!"

The other men cheer: "Huzzah! Huzzah!"

We turn our horses—Bev and me on our mare, Brandon, Daniel, and Elizabeth on their chestnut shorty—

and join the march. About two hundred yards in we come to General Washington, General Greene, and Captain Hamilton, all on horseback, all exhorting the men to keep pressing, boys, keep pressing. General Washington, as usual, is concerned, and of course he knows the whole attack is massively behind schedule, but it's such an impressive sight—a mile-long parade of men, horses, artillery—that maybe even the general feels a tad hopeful. There's too much going on at the moment for him to acknowledge us, but Captain Hamilton pulls up beside me.

"Have you . . . accomplished . . . what needed to be done?"

"We have not, Captain Hamilton."

"You have *not*?"

"No. Not yet."

"Then what is the danger?"

"General Washington's person. He must be protected at all times. We are going to scout ahead and make certain the path is safe, even if only fifty yards at a time."

"How . . . how would anyone else know the path we take?"

"That's a very good question. My guess is that our friend has been somehow *informed*. Don't ask me how."

"Informed? Of what?"

"Of the path we're taking."

"How could he know that?" Captain Hamilton asks. "We hardly know it ourselves."

"Like I said, don't ask me how. And I don't think we'll go wrong if we assume the worst."

He nods, and presses forward with his men. But then we are halted.

At the head of the line our leaders consult, orders are given, the word gets passed down, unit to unit, militia to militia. Half of us are going to the right, along River Road, under the command of General John Sullivan.

And half of us will go to the left, along Pennington Road, under the command of General Greene. Accompanying General Greene will be General Washington, General Henry Knox, who commands the cannons, Captain Alexander Hamilton, and all five of us.

SEVENTY-ONE

IT'S GOING TO TAKE us about four and a half hours to walk Pennington Road to Trenton.

It takes us maybe four and a half minutes to start arguing among ourselves again.

The horses are to blame. The mare and the chestnut shorty. Since there are only two of them and five of us, who rides when and with whom is the issue.

"We'll tire the horses," Bev says. "It should only be one rider at time. We can take turns."

Daniel concurs, and so does Brandon.

I don't. Seeing as how I don't know how to ride a horse, what it would mean for me is all walk, no ride.

I get outvoted. Three to one, with one abstention— Elizabeth. She says she'll walk, and won't ride alone.

I think she can. I don't think she wants to. Maybe she doesn't think it proper for a twelve-year-old girl to ride a horse alone, but Bev, of course, doesn't care what anyone thinks—she's riding.

So the next four and a half hours are only the worst time of my entire life. What makes it doubly worse is that Elizabeth walks besides me the entire time and doesn't complain at all.

Bev and Brandon and Daniel work out a rotation system, so two ride while one walks. When they walk with us they're way more cheerful than me, which doesn't help either.

At least I have sneakers. And socks. I think of that soldier I saw in MacDougall's New York Regiment who had nothing but rags wrapped twice around, with his black toes sticking out.

We can't just hunker down and endure the cold, the sleet, the snow, and the gale-force winds as best we can—no, we have to be on one hundred percent full *alert*. Which means keeping our heads up, our eyes wide, and our ears open.

Kramm could be anywhere. In a tree. Behind a bush or a shed. He would just need to step out, line up Washington, and fire.

But we see no sign of him, and the farther we go, the more I think: not here. *Not on this road. It will happen someplace else.*

Do you know how long four and a half hours is? Along

a crummy road in the dead of night in the middle of win-ter during a raging storm?

I bet you do not. And let me ask you this: when's the last time anyone you know walked from Pennington, New Jersey, to Trenton, New Jersey? It's nine miles.

No one walks that far any more, just to get from point A to point B. No one.

And these guys—our fellow winter patriots—have walked all the way from New York.

Washington rides, all the officers ride, but the men?

The men walk.

One lousy foot in front of the other.

With or without shoes.

And after the first or the second or the third hour I feel myself beginning to falter. I don't know how much longer I can hold up before I drop to the ground and let the entire Continental Army walk right over me.

But I don't. Elizabeth keeps me going, and so does Bev when it's her turn to walk. They don't give me *encouragement,* exactly—but the thought of pitching face-first into the snow in front of either one of them is just enough motivation to keep me going.

At some point it goes from being pitch-black to being not pitch-black to being somewhat not dark to being somewhat not too dark at all. If my brain were working properly, I'd recognize it as the dawn of a new day.

I can see stuff like trees, the road we're on, the soldiers, the sky.

The wind is still blowing, but a little less crazily, and the snow has stopped falling.

Then our parade is halted.

"My brave fellows," I hear someone say, and recognize the voice: General George Washington, commander in chief of the Continental Army of these United States.

"My brave fellows," General Washington says. And then he points his ungloved hand at a small sentry house down below.

Captain Hamilton and another officer ride stealthily down the hill, silently dismount from their horses, and draw their swords.

What happens next is a blur, a blur of blurs. We hear shouts and a scattering of chairs and tables. Then from the back of the house Hessians start running out, screaming at the top their lungs: *"Der Fiend! Der Fiend! Heraus! Heraus!"* Which means, "The enemy! The enemy! Out! Out!"

General Washington has heard enough. "Forward, men!" he yells. "Attack!"

SEVENTY-TWO

A ND THUS THE BATTLE OF TRENTON, whether or not I personally happen to be ready for it—which I'm not—begins.

Below us is the village of Trenton—not much more than a bunch of small wood houses—and at the beginning we don't see any Hessians. General Greene gets the men lined up, and General Knox, who commands the artillery, gets the cannons in place. General Washington sits atop his white steed, and if he's happy about how things are working out, he doesn't show it.

It's about eight o'clock in the morning. The Hessians are inside; whether they're sleeping one off or eating ham and eggs, it doesn't matter—they are not *outside*. They are not armed, ready, and *deployed*.

Rejoining us from River Road are General Sullivan's men. They line up on the high ground they're holding, though it's not as high as ours. You might not notice General Sullivan's men—if you're a Hessian, that is. You might stumble out, look up, and see, dead ahead, men and cannons. You'd be worried about that, all right, but at least you could see where the danger was.

And while you were looking straight ahead, you might just get cut to pieces by Sullivan's men to your left.

Which is exactly how it plays out.

General Washington nods, General Knox yells fire, and the cannons blow. Clouds of smoke pour from the cannons after each shot.

The noise alerts the Hessians, who come running into the street, armed, half-dressed, screaming, and mad.

We shoot at them from up top, and as they make their way forward, General Sullivan's men mow 'em down from the side.

It's a deadly crossfire. Smoke from the cannons and the muskets and rifles starts to obscure the battlefield, but we can see Hessians getting killed right in front of us, blood spattering. The Hessians aren't panicking, exactly, but they aren't counterattacking either. Their officers are yelling at them, trying to set up formations, but we've brought too much to bear. And General Knox keeps the cannons firing away.

Brandon and Daniel have joined in. Somehow they found a musket, and since Daniel knows how to load and fire the thing, they take turns. At this point, no one's shooting back.

Elizabeth and Bev have attached themselves to Captain Hamilton's cannon brigade and are passing cannonballs up the line.

I attach myself to a regiment of Virginians, and one of the soldiers thrusts a musket at me. "This one's too wet to fire," he says. "But the blade be true, boy, the blade be true!"

Then General Washington starts shouting above the din, "To the orchard, boys! To the orchard!" He jerks his head to the left. "I need men to follow me to the orchard!"

Every man in the Virginia regiment turns at once and starts running to the left.

Then we hear our general yell: "Charge, boys, charge with everything you've got!"

SEVENTY-THREE

SOME OF THE HESSIANS are now firing back. And in the orchard, which is about fifty yards to our left, they're even trying to set up cannons of their own. Three officers on horseback are shouting at the men in German. *"Macht schnell, macht schnell!"* I hear, which means "Hurry it up!"

But General Washington isn't going to give them a second. He rides over to the orchard, where we still have the high ground, and orders us to *charge.*

Not *fire.*

Charge.

Meaning, with our bayonets. With a great roar, we charge. Of course, I'm in the very last row. I'm not saying I'm afraid or anything. I just think the real soldiers ought to go first, you know?

There's maybe two hundred, three hundred of us, and we swarm down the high ground and into the Hessians. We charge, screaming like banshees, our muskets thrusting before us, and then something very remarkable happens.

Half the Hessians break ranks and *run*.

One of their officers, the one who seems to be in command, starts *screaming* at them, but then he gets shot in the stomach himself, probably by one of our sharpshooting riflemen, who love to pick off officers. The guy lets out a great *ooooof* and slumps on his horse. Two of his comrades rush to help him, but all the others keep running away.

The Virginians track down the fleeing Hessians, and use the bayonets as they were designed. It isn't pretty. The Hessians scream as cold steel is rammed through them.

Then General Washington, who is wading into the fray himself, has his horse, his great white steed, shot out from under him. He hardly skips a beat, though— his horse goes down, but he barely touches ground before he finds another horse and gets right on it. General Washington shouts orders, there is massive confusion, fireworks, cannon booms, musket shots, screams, Hessian officers yelling and Hessian soldiers running, and I am about one-half absolutely terrified and one-half desperate to find a Hessian myself. I think a cannonball from one of General Knox's artillery pieces whizzes by a few inches above our heads—*something* does, that's for sure—and then I see, out of the corner of my eye, something truly awful: a severed left arm. With a sword still in its fingers.

And then, nearly as fast as it started, it comes to an end.

The Hessian officer who had been shot in the stomach turns out to be their leader, a Colonel Johann Rall. Who is going to die, I know, in about two hours. I know this because I've read the history books; everyone else knows it from the looks of the man's pale, bloodless face. He's helped off his horse by two of his comrades and carried away.

The remaining Hessians wave white flags, General Washington holds up his hand, and just like that, all fighting ceases.

Smoke from the cannons and muskets drifts away, and the streets of Trenton are strewn now with rubble and bodies.

Brandon can't quite process this development. "Is that it?" Brandon asks. "It's over already?" His eyes are bulging, buggy. He's got the musket in his hands, bayonet attached—I think he was getting ready to charge himself.

"It's over, Brandon," I say. "We won."

"We won?"

"Of course we won. The Battle of Trenton, the Revolutionary War? Yes, Brandon. We wind up winning."

"I know that, dude. But, it only took like what—a half hour? Forty-five minutes?"

"Sometimes that's all it does take."

Brandon sighs and closes his eyes. "Man," he says. "I thought for sure I was going to be shot right in the head.

It was really scary. I kept thinking, *Am I going to get it now? Or now? Or now?*"

I nod at his bayonet, which only has snow on it. "So I guess you didn't have to use it," I say.

"No," he says. "But I was ready to."

"For a cause," I say. "Freedom."

"If you say so," says Brandon. He glances over the battlefield, where the injured Hessians are being helped by their brethren. "What was their cause?"

"I don't think they have one," I say. "They're professional soldiers, and go where they're sent. Look where it got 'em."

Brandon nods. "I just thought I'd be a little—you know—happier. Now that it's over."

"I'm happy," Daniel says, who's come to join us. "They're invaders. They don't belong in our country. I'll be even happier when we rid ourselves of all of them, Hessians and British."

Brandon puts his hand on Daniel's shoulder. "That's your fight, bro. All power to you. But us? Can we get out of here now, Mel? Can we go back to school?"

"How we going to do that, Brandon? There's that loose end, remember?"

"Oh, man. I forgot about that."

But I haven't. As a matter of fact, I'm starting to get a very weird feeling.

That something else is going to happen.

I just didn't think it was going to happen at the exact moment of Washington's greatest victory.

SEVENTY-FOUR

I TURN AROUND. AT THE top of the meadow, General George Washington is surveying the battlefield. He sits on his new horse. This must be a proud, and profound, moment for him. The Continental Army has not lost a single man. The Hessians have surrendered themselves and their position. If Washington survives, he'll lead this ragged army all the way to the defeat of the British Army, which is merely the world's most fearsome fighting force.

Notice I use the word *if.*

Because fifteen yards away from Washington is Butt-Ugly Kramm. Who has been waiting all this time for just this opportunity. *When everyone's guard is down.*

Brandon, Daniel, and I are maybe fifty yards away. I don't know where Bev is, or Elizabeth, or Captain Hamilton, or anyone else who can help.

And I can plainly see that no one, not for at least the next thirty seconds, will be able to get close enough to Washington to make a difference. Though it doesn't stop us from trying.

Or running.

Or shouting at the top of our lungs.

"General Washington! Watch it! On your left!"

Washington turns to his left, and so does Kramm. Which means Kramm's facing Brandon and me. He brings his right arm up, and fires.

Bam, bam, bam. Three shots. From the Luger he's been carrying around.

Two miss. One doesn't.

I know, because I hear a sickening *thud* and a gurgle of blood about two inches from my right ear.

Kramm crouches, turns back to Washington, raises his Luger, and is just about ready to squeeze off the rest of his rounds and change the course of history forever when his head is blasted to kingdom come.

It explodes like a watermelon. As I may have said before, I don't have to tell you what *that* looks like, do I?

Kramm had miscalculated: General Washington's men—his troops, his soldiers, his brothers—had him covered the whole time. They weren't *ever* going to allow their commander in chief to be cut down on the battlefield. One of the sharpshooting riflemen took out Kramm with a perfect shot.

The gurgling sound behind me? Kramm's shot missed me and hit an already wounded Hessian soldier who had just managed to get to his feet. He's keeled over, grabbing his shoulder. I don't think it will provide him much comfort to know that a German bullet did the damage.

Atop the hill, about thirty men come running over, and in a second Washington is surrounded by a protective phalanx.

So you could say a couple of things are going on here. It's one of those *moments* of total confusion and chaos when everyone knows something *huge* just happened, but no one's quite sure exactly *what*.

But I have to make sure I get to Kramm—or what's left of Kramm—before anyone else. First thing I do is grab his Luger, and stick it in the back of my pants.

Next to him is the leather satchel, with the initials T.G.W., INC. I take it.

Last thing I do is start walking away—at a very brisk pace—from General Washington, his men, and Kramm. I act like I'm going to be sick, because it's all too much for me.

After all, I'm just a kid, right?

SEVENTY-FIVE

THIRTY YARDS AWAY, WITH no one near me, I open up the leather satchel. Inside there's a bunch of stuff: papers, a pouch, three magazines for the Luger, a map, two Hershey bars, a compass, and a plastic first aid kit.

These are not items Daniel and Elizabeth are ever going to find at Ye Olde General Store.

I open up the pouch, and inside are maybe twenty or thirty coins.

I know what they are. Pure gold. You don't even have to be an expert. And they're also shiny and new, like they've just come from a store. On the front is a picture of an old dude with a beard. Around the edge it says SUID-AFRIKA * SOUTH AFRICA.

On the other side it says KRUGERRAND 2002 and there's a picture of a deer. Or maybe it's an antelope.

I open up a packet of papers. The first thing I see is a printed note. Two pages. Not handwritten, and most certainly not on parchment. On regular 8 ½-by-11-inch paper.

Kramm,

As promised, here is your first payment— twenty-five gold coins. These are pure gold. Pay no mind to the markings on the coins—they will fetch you what you want. Go to Philadelphia or New York City—find a bank, or if not a bank, a counting house—they will exchange these coins for currency, I promise you. When your job is done you will receive the rest of the payment— another 75 coins. You will be a very wealthy man, Kramm. Take care you spend your fortune wisely.

You will notice a weapon in this bag. It is called a Luger, and never you mind how it was manufactured or how I came to possess it. I give it to you, and, like the gold coins, you must use it wisely. I'm sure you will be able to handle this, but I have included a diagram of this weapon and some brief operating instructions. Its virtue is that it need not be loaded each time you wish to fire. It has what is called a magazine, or a cartridge, of nine bullets, which you insert in the butt end of the pistol. I have included three extra magazines. This should be more than enough to accomplish your mission.

You will find Washington across the river with his troops. I have included a map which gives you his precise location, plus additional maps which detail the route he intends to take to Trenton. Your first objective is to eliminate Washington prior to his crossing the Delaware, which is his plan. If that fails, your secondary objective is to eliminate Washington at some other point in the proceedings, but UNDER NO CIRCUMSTANCES MUST WASHINGTON BE ALLOWED TO DECLARE VICTORY AND RETURN TO PENNSYLVANIA. I will leave the exact method of this elimination up to you, but bear in mind that Washington is not exactly the most intelligent general who's ever lived. He has a weakness for horses—maybe you could find some to sell him and lure him to his demise. But the method doesn't matter as much as the result.

Finally, you will notice a compass, which I'm sure you know how to use, and also a special treat, which you may have ONLY after you complete the job. I've included two. They are called Hershey bars. Soldiers around the world have come to love them. When you have succeeded in your mission, open up and take a bite—I guarantee you will love it.

One last thing, Kramm: don't fail.

If you fail, I will track you down, and make sure you regret it for the rest of your life. Which will not be for long.

Sincerely,
Kurtis
President, Things Go Wrong, Inc.

SEVENTY-SIX

READ IT AGAIN.

And then another time.

After that, I recheck the stuff in the bag. I feel like eating the Hershey bars, but something tells me that just might be the last thing I'd ever eat.

I pick up the gold coins. I look at the maps, which are perfectly laid out, easy to read, and show precise locations and routes.

President, Things Go Wrong, Inc.?

What the heck is that all about?

"Mel?" I hear behind me.

I turn my head. Bev, Daniel, and Elizabeth are standing ten feet away. They must have followed me across the battlefield. Daniel and Elizabeth are grim, but seem determined; Bev, on the other hand, seems a little shell-shocked.

"Are you okay, Mel?" Bev asks. "We heard that you . . . that you . . ."

"Were taken ill," says Elizabeth.

"I'm fine," I say. "Considering." I check over the scene: our guys are rounding up their guys. Our generals are still on horseback, shouting out orders; their generals are walking with their heads down, ashamed.

About a dozen houses have had their roofs torn up or their front doors blasted through or all their windows broken—the owners won't be happy when they find out. Debris is strewn everywhere: broken bags of flour, scattered remains of food, pieces of furniture, mismatched planks of wood, pieces of roofs, and other sorts of unidentifiable junk.

"How about you guys?" I ask. "Bev?"

"It was horrible," Bev says. "Absolutely horrible. I'm not sure I can . . . I know how to . . ."

"Deal with it?"

"Yes."

"Think of the cause, Bev. Think of the results."

"This will be a lesson to them," Elizabeth says, glaring. "When we put our minds to it, we shan't be stopped. They'd best leave, the British, and take their Hessians with them. They'll never conquer us. Never."

"Elizabeth," I say. "I have a feeling that you're one hundred percent right about that. But our job is done here. Anybody seen Brandon? We can't go till we find him."

"We're going?" says Bev.

"You're going?" says Daniel.

"We have to," I say. "Once we're all together." I hold up Kramm's leather satchel. "I found some interesting stuff. Pieces to the puzzle, you might say. We'll take it back with us and figure things out."

"Back?" says Daniel. "Back where?"

"Back home. Our home. Now—when's the last time anyone saw Brandon?"

Daniel raises his hand, points down the hill. "Your Brandon went that way. He said he needed to find something."

"Find what?"

"He didn't say."

"Oh brother." I start down the hill. "Let's go," I say. "Bev, from here on in we all stay together. And we only have one last thing to do: locate Brandon. Then we can get out of here."

We begin walking. Our Continentals are lining up Hessian prisoners, and going through the houses they used for barracks. But no Brandon among them.

Below us is a bridge. It's at the bottom of a sloping hill, past the battlefield and beyond the small number of buildings that constitute the city of Trenton. It's a stone bridge, and it crosses a meandering stream called the Assunpink Creek. The Hessians could have retreated across the bridge instead of staying to fight. Could have, but didn't.

Brandon is in the middle of the bridge.

Leading the mare and the chestnut shorty that brought us here.

"Brandon!" I say. "What are you doing?"

"Getting the horses, dude. We told that guy we'd bring 'em back, remember?"

"How did they get across the bridge?"

"Must have run when the shooting started. Horses get scared, you know, and don't know what to do. Just like people sometimes."

He stops. Brandon's face isn't right, though. He's usually kind of goofy, if you want to know the truth. Never serious.

Except now.

"What's the matter?"

"Nothing."

"Come on, Brandon. What's the matter?"

"Well, it's just that . . . these horses? I really couldn't let them get away. It's been on my mind. After what we put them through? We rode 'em all night in the blizzard. And I don't know when they've last eaten."

"Well, you got them. So we've done all we can. It's time. For us. You know. To go back."

Brandon gives each horse a nose rub. "I don't know, Mel."

"You don't know about what?"

"About going back. To school? Term papers? Tests and quizzes? Maybe I should stay. Take my chances."

"Come on. Don't be ridiculous."

"Why's it so ridiculous, Mel? I might not even make

it out of the sixth grade. I think I'm pretty much failing everything."

"That's because you don't even try, Brandon."

"No, it's because I don't even care, Mel. I tell you what I do care about, though: horses. Too bad I can't go . . . you know. Home."

"You mean, like New Mexico home, right?"

"Right. We used to have horses, on our ranch. Then everything changed. You know. When my mom started to get all . . . kind of weird."

"I know. Bev should be in California with her mom. I should be with my parents in New York. But . . . what are we going to do, Brandon? They don't call us 'left behind' for nothing."

"What we can do is we stay behind on our own. Not some place they dump us."

"We all go, Brandon. Or we all stay."

"Says who?"

"Says me."

"And who elected you, Mel? I don't remember there being a vote."

"You can't stay, Brandon. This is the *past,* for crying out loud. What do you think you're going to do ten years from now? Twenty? Think about it."

"You and Bev can go. I'm staying."

"What about us, Brandon? What if the phones have to be programmed for the same time? Then maybe it won't work for any of us, and we'll all be stuck here."

"How could you know that?"

"'Cause I worked on the thing. Dr. Franklin helped me, remember?"

"So Benjamin Franklin told you we all have to go? At the same time?"

"He didn't, but I bet he would. Whether the app works that way or not. He'd say we all have to hang together, because if we don't, we'll hang separately. He was talking about all the guys who signed the Declaration of Independence, but it goes for us too, just the same."

Brandon doesn't agree, but he doesn't disagree either. Instead he scratches the horse again, and both of them nuzzle closer.

"They have horses in New Jersey, Brandon," I say. "Even today."

"I know. It's just that I never get near any."

"So maybe we can do something about that, okay?"

"Okay," he says. "When?"

"As soon as possible. But first, there's another thing: see this?" I show him Kramm's satchel. "I think there's a lot more to it than just this. Kramm isn't the only bad guy. There's a bigger bad guy who goes by the name of Kurtis. We're going to need to figure out who he is and what he's up to before . . . before stuff happens. Or doesn't happen, as the case may be. So this might not be our last adventure."

I finally got his attention. I'm trying every trick I have, because I know I'd never forgive myself if we left Brandon behind.

It would be kind of . . . un-American, wouldn't it?

SEVENTY-SEVEN

"COME ON, MAN," I say. "Let's go. Can I take one of these? Maybe you can teach me how to ride a horse someday. It could come in handy."

Brandon hands me the reins to the mare. I give her a tug, and together we all walk back across the bridge. Bev and Daniel and Elizabeth are waiting.

"We good?" says Bev.

"We're good," I say.

"So that's it? We can go?"

"Pretty much. We have to make sure the horses get back to their owner, though, right, Brandon?" I shift my eyes to Daniel and Elizabeth, and scratch my chin. "If we could only find two people who could use a ride back."

Brandon hands them the reins. "See if you can find

them something to eat," he says. "They're probably starving."

"As are we," says Elizabeth, and takes the reins. "But we shall do what we can."

Someone shouts at us from up the slope. It's Captain Hamilton. "Let's go!" he shouts. "We're heading up the road we came down!"

"Already?" says Daniel.

"I'm afraid so," I say. "General Washington doesn't like it here. He thinks the entire Continental Army is too exposed. He won't rest until everyone's safely in Pennsylvania."

"He must be mad," says Elizabeth. "We couldn't possibly walk that far. We're too exhausted."

"Maybe so. But he's going to make you. That's why he's in charge."

"Are you privy to the general's thinking?" says Elizabeth.

"Kind of," I say. "I'm privy to history, is more like it."

"Hurry!" says Captain Hamilton. "You do not wish to be left behind, do you?"

No, sir. We do not. But this trip is not one Bev or Brandon or I will be taking.

We walk up the slope to Captain Hamilton, who is in a very big hurry. I think some of the Continentals—probably MacDougall's New York Regiment—have found something besides Hessians and boxes of ammunition. Rum, namely. Things are starting to get a little rowdy.

"We must leave," says Captain Hamilton. "We are to return to Pennsylvania without delay."

"Understood," I say. "Daniel and Elizabeth will join you, and bring back these horses. The three of us will . . . um . . . have other plans."

Captain Hamilton looks me directly in the eye. "Are you quite certain?"

"We are. We will not be troubling you again. All will be well, Captain Hamilton. Trust us. From here on out."

"Very well," Captain Hamilton says. "Good luck to you." He then rejoins his men.

They are nearly done forming the return column. It's ragged, but orderly enough: 2,400 brave Americans, a thousand or so Hessian prisoners, six German cannons, cartloads of food, an ammunition wagon, and even a Hessian marching band. Then the whole thing starts to move out. They're going to have to go back along the half-frozen and totally rutted roads they came in on, but this time they'll be marching not as rebels, but as victors.

Next is Daniel and Elizabeth's turn.

"Goodbye, Daniel," I say, and shake his hand. "Goodbye, Elizabeth," I say, and shake her hand as well. I don't think kissing or hugging members of the opposite sex—especially those who haven't been properly introduced to your parents—is something she's quite ready for. So I don't try. She takes my hand, and gives me a very delicate shake.

"I think you ought to stay," says Elizabeth. "We've

unfinished business. The British are quite far from being defeated."

"That is true," I say. "But you will prevail."

"How can you be so certain?"

"I know. Believe me. But we don't belong here, Elizabeth. Our mission is complete. Nothing good will come from overstaying our welcome."

Daniel and Bev shake hands, and Brandon says his goodbyes. Then Daniel gets astride the chestnut shorty, and Elizabeth gets on the mare. "I do know how to ride," she says, "and I will, whether anyone likes it or not." Then the both of them are off.

That only leaves General George Washington. We make our way up the street, and there he is, astride his horse, yelling at his men to hurry.

It doesn't take long. "General Washington," I say. "We must leave now. Every success imaginable will be yours. We thank you for the privilege of serving."

"You enlisted?" he says.

"Kinda sorta," I say. "But not really. Speaking of enlistments, I know your men have only another week before their time is up. You're going to need an army, General. Especially now. You might get another six weeks or so out of your men, if you ask."

"So I shall," he says. "So I shall. Well then. Off with you, and Godspeed." He doesn't offer to shake our hands. Instead, he gives us a salute, and we salute him back.

Then he goes up the hill, joins his men, and disappears.

SEVENTY-EIGHT

THE FIRST THING I do when all the troops are gone is show Bev and Brandon the leather satchel. "Check this out," I say, and point to the initials stenciled on the bag: T.G.W., INC. "I have Kramm's bag." They peek in, see the extra Luger magazines, the Hershey bars, the maps. I read Kurtis's note aloud.

"Who is Kurtis?" Bev says.

"You mean, who is Kurtis besides being the president of Things Go Wrong, Inc.? I have no idea who he is exactly, but I think I know what he's up to."

"Which is what?"

"I think he's the dude who invented the iTime app. Do you remember what it says when you open it up? That thing about "the aim is to play, to mess about, who says

325

things have to be this way and not another?" Remember that?"

"Kind of," says Bev. "What do you think it means?"

"I don't know if I want to tell you what I'm thinking, Bev," I say. "'Cause what I'm thinking is pretty weird. Though I'm pretty sure I'm right."

"Mel has a theory," says Brandon. "Don't you, Mel? What is it?"

"Like I said, it'll sound weird."

"Out with it, Mel," Bev says. "What could be weirder than anything else we've gone through in the last twenty-four hours?"

"You have a point," I say. "All right, here goes: this guy Kurtis? I think he invented the iTime app for one thing—to go back in history and screw things up."

"That doesn't make any sense," Bev says. "Why would anyone want to do that?"

"Just for the fun of it," says Brandon, as if he understands Kurtis perfectly, and maybe he does. "Just because everything seems so . . . so . . . perfect."

It doesn't make a bit of sense to me. But then I remember this birthday party I was invited to when I was about six or seven. It was at a Chuck E. Cheese's, and everyone was going haywire. Then a kid named Alfred, who was going bonkers with all the noise and commotion, decided to tip over the birthday cake.

Everyone screamed.

Except Alfred, who laughed like a hyena. He had just

ruined the party, and nothing could have made him happier.

"All right, guys," I say. "You ready? I think we should stand in a circle." We all take out our iPhones and tap on the iTime icon.

"Make sure the date is changed," I say. "To yesterday. Christmas Day, remember? But put in the right year."

Everyone puts in the right date, and the right time. To make sure, I go around and check. "On the count of three," I say. "We're going to hit the *Submit* button, okay?"

"Okay," says Bev.

"Roger," says Brandon.

I count down. We hit *Submit* and stare at our screens. Then, the magic begins.

The spinning thing first. Then it feels like we're going up a long, long roller coaster in the dark. And finally we come crashing down, until we land, with a thump, thump, thump, in the basement of the general store.

In our own time.

We can tell. The first thing we see is the MacBook that got us here in the first place.

The second thing we see is Mr. Hart, our teacher and present-to-past texter.

And the third thing is the old man. The one we noticed before, scurrying away from the basement of the general store. Now he's stooped over the MacBook, clacking away on the keyboard, and he seems very, very annoyed.

SEVENTY-NINE

"**I**T'S ABOUT TIME," the old man says, glaring at us.

Mr. Hart rushes forward and nearly knocks us over, he's so happy. Bev is definitely not in any mood to be hugged. Same deal with Brandon and me. But I guess from Mr. Hart's point of view, it kind of fits the occasion. We've only been missing for, like, over two hundred years.

Once the hugs are out of the way, it doesn't take long for Mr. Hart to go from relieved to aggrieved. "Guys, are you kidding? I was scared out of my mind. Do you have any idea what could have happened to me? I could have lost my job, for starters. And then there's no telling what misery your parents could have put me through."

"We're happy to see you too, Mr. Hart," Bev says. "How's your day going?"

"Awful," says Mr. Hart. "Most incredibly awful. It's not every day you lose three kids . . . just like that."

"It wasn't," says the old man, "just like that. One of you must have done something to this computer. It was set up perfectly—just not for any of you."

"And you are who?" says Brandon.

"This is Professor Moncrieff," says Mr. Hart. "He worked very closely with Albert Einstein, at Princeton. Professor Moncrieff has invented an application that is able to transport people through a tunnel in the space-time continuum. I think you may be familiar with it."

"Oh yeah," I say.

"I'm not sure I really believed," Mr. Hart says, "that such a thing could even *work*."

"Of course it worked," Professor Moncrieff says. "Have I not explained it to you, Mr. Hart? Have I not allowed you to *text* your student there, of all things?"

"Well, yes, you did," says Mr. Hart. "But . . ."

"But nothing," Professor Moncrieff interrupts. "I have spent the last thirty-five years of my life seeing to it that it would work. And, if I do say so myself, it worked to perfection. Now tell me: Physically, do you feel disoriented? Nauseated? Light-headed?"

"I feel hungry," says Brandon.

"I feel like I could use a shower," says Bev.

"Never mind any of that! My observations are that you are all intact, and in perfect working order. Now then: who messed about with the computer?"

Two of us take a step to the rear, leaving Brandon up front, and alone.

"Why is this not surprising," says Mr. Hart.

"I thought there would have been some kind of password," Brandon says. "I just started hitting some keys to get the thing to wake up. How was I to know it would send us back in time?"

"You couldn't have," Professor Moncrieff says. "That much is certain. But why were you in this basement? It is the only place I could find on such short notice that had an available supply of electricity."

"Fooling around," Brandon admits. "We were upstairs and saw you leave. And we wondered what you were doing down here . . . and you know."

"One thing led to another?"

"Exactly."

"Wait a minute," I say. "Wait just a minute here. Who is Kurtis? And just what is Things Go Wrong, Inc.? Are you part of that?"

"Calm down, Mel," Mr. Hart says. "There's no reason to fly off the handle."

"No reason to fly off the handle? There's *every* reason to fly off the handle. How do you explain this?" I show them Kramm's leather satchel, with the initials T.G.W., INC. stenciled on the side. "Do you know what he did? This guy Kurtis? He *paid* a guy to assassinate General George Washington!"

"You didn't mention that," Mr. Hart says.

"Of course I did not!" Professor Moncrieff says. "Do you think I'm stupid? Do you think I would trust you or any man with information like that? The very point of this entire exercise has been in jeopardy the moment these . . . these . . . these *children* interfered with my computer!"

"Mr. Hart, we need to call the police," I say. "This guy is trying to mess around with . . . with *history* itself!"

"Not I!" roars Professor Moncrieff. "Not I, you *child*! I am attempting to save history, not destroy it! And you lousy kids are getting in my way!"

"Tell it to the cops," Bev says. "I'm sure they'll love to hear it."

"Don't call anyone!" Professor Moncrieff shouts. "Especially not the police! They cannot be trusted! I warn you! You do not know the danger!"

"We almost got our heads shot off," Brandon says. "So we know all about danger. Let's give him two minutes, guys. He explains everything or we call the police."

Professor Moncrieff manages to take a deep breath and closes his eyes for second, as if he's trying to keep a lid on it.

He's old. I mean, *way* old. He's got the stoop, the liver spots, the wrinkles, the snow-white hair, the huge ears—but his eyes are as sharp as anyone's. They're dull blue, those eyes. They narrow their focus a little. Then become hard as cobalt.

"Well. I will explain this much to you: I was a very

young man when I studied with Dr. Einstein. And he himself was a very young man when he made his most important discoveries regarding the nature of time. I only fleshed out his ideas, carried them to their logical, if extreme, conclusions. You are by now familiar with the app called iTime. I am its intellectual father, but, sadly, only its co-inventor. I required the services of an advanced programmer. I did not, unfortunately, possess the necessary—how is it phrased these days—the necessary *skill set.*"

"Okay," I say. "And?"

"And what?" says Professor Moncrieff.

"Well, are you going to tell us why we were zapped back to 1776?"

"No. This is classified information."

"Classified by the *government*?"

"Classified by *me,* young man. I don't trust the government. Never have. Never will."

"You have to tell us more than that. We only just risked our lives to save George Washington. We did it, by the way. In case anyone is wondering."

"And you're welcome," says Bev. "Boys, let's call the cops. He hasn't told us a thing."

Professor Moncrieff holds up a hand. "Very well," he says. "It is my co-inventor who has betrayed us. It is the Kurtis you speak of. He decided our program was worth somewhat more than what I could pay him. Kurtis has gone, as they say, off the deep end. Quite a bit off. He has stolen the code for the iTime app."

"And not only that," I say. "He also formed a company: Things Go Wrong, Inc. Of which he is the president."

"And the sole employee," Professor Moncrieff says. "He intends to make a billion dollars. Or possibly ten billion dollars. Among other things."

"How is he going to make a billion dollars?" Bev asks.

"Two ways. He can sell iTime to anyone who is willing to pay, and they can do what they wish with it. And second, Kurtis believes that he stands to profit if he can rearrange the *outcome* of things. He can place *bets,* if you will. On an outcome that will be entirely of his own making. But most dangerous of all, Kurtis is not *primarily* motivated by money. He merely requires a great deal of money to further his most fundamental desire. Kurtis is, I fear, a practitioner of the darkest art of them all."

"You mean, like, witchcraft?" says Brandon.

"No. I mean *chaos theory.* He is the world's foremost expert, and now very unfortunately, he is putting into practice what he has long contemplated in theory."

"Chaos theory?" says Bev. "What in the world is that?"

"Technically, it is the study of dynamic systems. You may have heard of the famous example—an extra flap of a butterfly's wings in Asia could alter a weather system by the tiniest amount—but enough to cause, ultimately, a hurricane of gargantuan proportions on the other side of the world. Kurtis, alas, is not interested in experimenting with butterflies. He requires a figure of consequence. From his perspective, George Washington is a very suitable candidate."

"He left a note," I say, pointing to Kramm's satchel.

"Very typical. Kurtis is starved for attention. He, un-like me, was not willing to labor for decades in obscurity. But what Kurtis doesn't know is that I have inserted spy-ware into his copy of the source code. So I am able to track the movements of anyone who uses the iTime app. I was quite aware, therefore, of Kurtis's activities. Once I learned where Kurtis programmed his iTime app, it was not difficult to guess his intentions. Kurtis himself went back in time in order to secure a *change agent*. Or, in other words, someone to do his dirty work."

"Kramm," I say.

"The ugly German dude," says Brandon.

"I am assuming," Professor Moncrieff says, "that you have met the change agent."

"Yep," I say. "Things didn't work out so well for him."

"Wait a minute here," says Mr. Hart. "Hold on. Has anyone thought through the *risk* of all this?"

"Do you mean the risk of doing nothing?" says Profes-sor Moncreiff.

"I mean the risk of sending . . . children . . . into an incredibly dangerous situation!"

"They interfered," Professor Moncrieff says. "They admit to it themselves. They stuck their noses where they didn't belong. It is entirely their fault. I had other plans to . . . remedy the situation. I had assembled a team. Of *men*. Not kids. Men with specialized, shall we say, abili-ties. Ex–Navy Seal. Ex-CIA. Ex–Army Ranger. They were nearly ready to be . . . inserted into the deployment zone. Then? You kids interfered with my plans!"

"Well, we *kids* remedied it for you," Bev says.

"Yeah," says Brandon. "When we last saw him, George Washington was alive and well."

"They crossed the Delaware," I say. "They won at Trenton. So all's well that ends well, right?"

"Right," says Bev. "Now I just want to get out of here. I need a hot shower in the worst way."

"You will be free to go in a minute. In any case, from this point forward, further information is classified. Know that Kurtis is a most relentless man, however. Most relentless. He no doubt will make other . . . arrangements. Please now give me your phones. They must be deprogrammed."

Now, this I'm not expecting.

Give up our phones? After what we've been through with them?

I check with Brandon. I check with Bev.

Bev shakes her head *no*.

No.

On this one we most definitely have a united front. As our self-proclaimed leader, I step up, so I'm standing directly in front of this Professor Moncrieff guy. I look him dead in the eye. "That's not going to happen," I say. "Not in a thousand years."

This is a very satisfying thing to say, and I mean every word. I feel good about myself, even. I stood up to The Man.

But Professor Moncrieff only smiles. A very crooked smile. Then he snaps his fingers, and the door to the basement opens.

Three men step in.

Men.

Not kids. Military-type dudes. Each one is maybe six-foot-two and 220 pounds. Hands as big as waffle irons. Close-cropped hair. Shades. Arms crossed, like they mean *business.*

This must be the team he was telling us about. The one he assembled.

"A thousand years?" Professor Moncrieff says. "These days it just doesn't mean as much as it used to, does it?"

Uh-oh. Maybe we haven't come to the end after all.

AUTHOR'S NOTE

I have to confess that although I've tried to stick pretty close to the historical record of Washington's Crossing of the Delaware, I've taken a few "liberties" here and there. The biggest one involves Ben Franklin. I really wanted to include Ben because I think he's such a wonderful character, and besides, who else would be able to recharge an iPhone? The real Ben Franklin was not in Philadelphia in December 1776, however; he had in fact made it to France, where he bedazzled all of Paris as the lead representative from the Continental Congress. Other than this, I don't think I've made other deliberate variations in the timeline or the events of the crossing itself, although as a fiction writer I have certainly made up scenes that never occurred.

The portrayal of both Ben Franklin and George Washington are my own interpretations, but I hope my admiration comes through. Certainly each man wasn't perfect, but what strikes me most about them is how much they risked to help create a new nation. Ben and George were successful, prominent men who could have kept their heads down and played it safe—but didn't. The risk wasn't simply losing an election or having a piece of legislation voted down, either. Had the British prevailed, they would have been prosecuted as traitors, or simply hanged from the nearest tree. On the other hand, both men knew full well that if the revolution succeeded, they would be remembered—and honored—throughout history. The stakes were as high as they get.

I grew up a few miles from George Washington's headquarters in Morristown, New Jersey, where he spent the winter of 1779–1780, and it must have been from passing by the place so often that I first developed my love of American history. I was a curious kid and liked to find things out, which sometimes meant I had to read books and go to the library. (I would have been *all* over Wikipedia had it been around!) I learned that if you have sharp eyes, you can notice stuff. Scattered throughout New Jersey are dozens of historical markers that trace Washington's routes and pathways along the grid of today's highly developed road system. Although New Jersey surely has many more highways, bridges, buildings, golf courses, and industrial complexes than it did two hundred years ago, beneath all that we have the same land, the same rivers and streams, the same hills and ridges, and the same ocean. Fewer trees, perhaps. Well, definitely fewer trees.

By the time my wife, Cindy, and I had our own children, I was eager to show them what I knew of Washington's travels within our state, and in a process of mutual discovery we began exploring the realm around us. I think we must have gone to our first reenactment of Washington Crossing the Delaware when my oldest son, Thomas, was six and his brother, Charlie, was three. It was a beautiful Christmas afternoon, cold but bright and clear, and I distinctly remember asking myself, as I looked out upon the thousands that had gathered for the occasion, what would *we* do if we were suddenly transported back to 1776? Would we have the same courage, the same resolve, as Washington and his troops? Could any of us modern-day citizens endure what our forefathers endured?

Thus an idea for a novel was born, although the research took about ten years. During that period I tried to read, see, and experience as much as I could of Washington's Crossing. I'm afraid I cajoled Thomas and Charlie to join me as wingmen as we traced the foot route from the landing to Trenton, saw reenactments of the Battle of Trenton and the Battle of Princeton, and poked our noses into backyards and byways along the route that we hoped might still retain important, and heretofore undiscovered, evidence of the journey. So far we haven't found anything, but we're still looking.

DP, Pennington, NJ

RECOMMENDED READING

Allen, Thomas B. *George Washington, Spymaster: How the Americans Outspied the British and Won the Revolutionary War.* Washington, DC: National Geographic Children's Books, 2004.

Freedman, Russell. *Give Me Liberty! The Story of the Declaration of Independence.* New York: Holiday House, 2000.

Fritz, Jean. *And Then What Happened, Paul Revere?* New York: Putnam & Grosset, 1996.

———. *What's the Big Idea, Ben Franklin?* New York: Putnam & Grosset, 2001.

Hale, Nathan. *Nathan Hale's Hazardous Tales: One Dead Spy.* New York: Amulet Books, 2012.

Lawson, Robert. *Ben and Me: An Astonishing Life of Benjamin Franklin by His Good Mouse Amos.* New York: Little, Brown, 1939.

McGovern, Ann. *The Secret Soldier: The Story of Deborah Sampson.* New York: Scholastic, 1990.

Murphy, Jim. *The Crossing: How George Washington Saved the American Revolution.* New York: Scholastic Press, 2010.

Murray, Stuart. *The American Revolution* (DK Eyewitness Books). New York: DK Children, 2010.

Raum, Elizabeth. *The Revolutionary War: An Interactive History Adventure.* New York: Capstone Press, 2009.

Schanzer, Rosalyn. *George vs. George: The American Revolution as Seen from Both Sides.* Washington, DC: National Geographic Children's Books, 2004.

Sheinkin, Steve. *King George: What Was His Problem? The Whole Hilarious Story of the American Revolution.* New York: Square Fish, 2009.

WEBSITES OF INTEREST

GEORGE WASHINGTON

Letters of George Washington, University of Virginia
(gwpapers.virginia.edu)

Meet George Washington, Mount Vernon estate
(www.mountvernon.org/georgewashington/facts)

All About George Washington, White House
(whitehouse.gov/about/presidents/georgewashington)

Washington's World, A Game for Kids, MountVernon.org
(washingtonsworld.org)

All About the War of Independence, Smithsonian
(amhistory.si.edu/militaryhistory/printable/section.asp?id=1)

The Smithsonian's History Explorer: The American Revolution
(historyexplorer.si.edu/themes/theme/?key=123)

The American Revolution (theamericanrevolution.org)

BENJAMIN FRANKLIN

Ben Franklin, PBS (pbs.org/benfranklin)

Ben's Guide to the U.S. Government for Kids
(bensguide.gpo.gov/benfranklin)

REVOLUTIONARY WAR

A Timeline of the Revolution, PBS
(pbs.org/ktca/liberty/chronicle_timeline.html)

Road to Revolution Quiz, PBS (pbs.org/ktca/liberty/road.html)

Revolutionary War Maps, Library of Congress
(memory.loc.gov/ammem/gmdhtml/armhtml/armhome.html)

EARLY AMERICAN HISTORY

America's Story from America's Library, Library of Congress
(americaslibrary.gov)

Archiving Early America: Your Window Into America's
Founding Years (earlyamerica.com)

FOUNDING DOCUMENTS

Transcript of the Declaration of Independence
(archives.gov/exhibits/charters/declaration.html)

Transcript of the Constitution
(archives.gov/exhibits/charters/constitution.html)

Transcript of the Bill of Rights
(archives.gov/exhibits/charters/bill_of_rights.html)

REENACTMENTS AND LIVING HISTORY

The **Washington Crossing Historic Park** hosts an annual memorial re-creation of Washington Crossing the Delaware River. A dress rehearsal of the Crossing occurs in early December, and the "official" Crossing occurs each Christmas Day at approximately 1:00 pm. Located at 1112 River Road in Washington Crossing, Pennsylvania. For more information, visit ushistory.org /washingtoncrossing.

Living history programs about the Revolutionary War are ongoing at the **Old Barracks Museum**, located at 101 Barrack Street, in Trenton, New Jersey. For more information, visit barracks.org.

There is a reenactment of the **Battle of Monmouth** each June in Tennent, New Jersey. Sponsored by the Friends of Monmouth Battlefield, Inc. For more information, visit friendsofmonmouth .org/index.html.

Reenactment and living history events take place annually at **Fort Ticonderoga** in New York. Reenactments have included the 1775 Capture of Fort Ticonderoga, American Soldiers Retreat by Bateaux to Ticonderoga, and the 1777 Capture of Fort Ticonderoga. For more information, visit fortticonderoga.org.

A reenactment of the **Battle of Great Bridge** is held annually on the first Saturday in December at the Great Bridge in Chesapeake, Virginia. For more information, visit virginia.org /Listings/Events/BattleofGreatBridge.

A **Revolutionary War Reenactment Festival** takes place each fall at Mount Harmon in Earleville, Maryland. For more information, visit mountharmon.org/events.html.

The **Brigade of the American Revolution** is a nonprofit organization that reenacts the life and time period of soldiers of the Revolutionary War. For more information and a list of events, visit brigade.org.

The **Continental Line, Inc.** is a nonprofit organization based in Pennsylvania that reenacts events from the Revolutionary War. For more information and a list of events, visit continentalline .org.

The **Northwest Territory Alliance** (NWTA) is a Midwest-based nonprofit reenactment organization. For more information and a list of events, visit nwta.com.

ACKNOWLEDGMENTS

Thank you to Brian DeFiore, the best agent in town, and to Phoebe Yeh, the best editor in town. I was on the outside looking in for a long time—a *very* long time—until the stars aligned and I got a double dose of tremendous good luck. I simply can't imagine this book without the combined efforts of Brian and Phoebe.

At Crown Books for Young Readers, thanks to Rachel Weinick for her kind assistance, to the copyediting team of Nancy Elgin and Alison Kolani, who didn't let me get away with anything, and to Ken Crossland and C. F. Payne for the cover design and art.

Thanks to my sons, Thomas and Charlie, for accompanying me on our excursions and for listening to long-winded history lessons at the dinner table. Thanks to my mother, Ginny Potter, whose efforts on her daily newspaper column (called "The Potter's Wheel") provided the genesis for my earliest literary aspirations. Thanks to my brother, Bruce Potter, who helped when it was needed the most, and for whom no idea is too outlandish. Thanks also to my late aunt Elizabeth Potter and my cousin Susan McVicar for critical support along the way. To Chuck Amsterdam for the laughs every Monday at lunch, and to Alan Shoemake, friend and photographer, for doing the best with what he had.

Thanks most especially to my wife, Cindy, who has been with me on this journey from the start. I don't think she ever doubted the outcome, even when I did.